RED JACK

ALSO BY ALEX LINWOOD

The Jack of Magic Series

Red Jack

Moss Gate

Black Raid

Iron War

THE JACK OF MAGIC BOOK 1

RED JACK

ALEX LINWOOD

GREENLEES
PUBLISHING

This is a work of fiction. Names, characters, organizations, places, events, and incidents are either products of the author's imagination or are used fictitiously. Any resemblance to actual persons, living or dead, or actual events is purely coincidental.

Published by Greenlees Publishing, contact@greenleespublishing.com

ISBN-13: 978-1-951098-09-4

Cover design by Dominic Forbes

Hare emblem courtesy of Lisa Parker | www.lisaparker.co.uk

For Adventurers Everywhere

Portia looked down at the harbor where the royal courier ship of Coverack was at anchor. The maroon and gold banner hung over the side announcing its royal status, as if the rich mahogany of its sleek sides and perfectly scrubbed decks were not an announcement enough. It stood in stark contrast to the faded gray wood of the fishing vessels that filled the harbor. She wondered what the royal ship was doing in Valencia and tried to imagine what it would be like to be a member on board, entitled to announce oneself, instead of a lowly orphan thief trying to survive hidden on the streets.

She was paying so little attention that she accidentally walked into a merchant who was dressed head to toe in rich red velvet. A gasp escaped Portia as she bounced off his large belly. He glared at her as she mumbled an apology and tried to duck away from him. She did not want him to get a good look at her face. But he was determined to see her. Portia's face reddened as she bowed even further and turned her face away as she backed up. A few curious onlookers watched. Portia's hands curled into fists of frustration at her own mistake. If she wasn't careful, and failed to follow her own rules of thieving, she would get caught. Worse yet, Mark would get caught. Luckily, the merchant was satisfied with her embarrassment and turned away. Portia exhaled softly.

She glanced down the road to the pastry chef's stall where she had sent Mark. He wasn't as skilled at pickpocketing as she was, so she had sent him to where the harried mothers usually were—those women who were trying to juggle children, bags of groceries, and money—and who were usually easy marks for losing track of at least one of those items. He was small for his eleven years, and could easily pass for a misplaced child, especially if he took care to wash the dirt from his face. The harbor market was unusually crowded today. The throngs of people made it hard to see him. Perhaps the crowds had something to do with the courier ship. Maybe others were just as curious as she was and had come to see if they could find out anything themselves.

Portia moved closer to the pastry stall. This time she was more careful in her passage, weaving between people and doing her best at being invisible. Invisibility wasn't a magical ability that she had, but it was amazing how close being poor and dirty was to actually being invisible. No one wanted to notice her, so they didn't. She saw Mark leaning casually against a rain barrel, keeping his face down. His eyes flickered up at her when she approached him, and he reached out a hand and grabbed her, pulling her close.

"Don't look around," he said quietly. "There are Brown

Hares by the ale seller. At least they have the mark of that gang." He twisted his body so his back was to the ale sellers. "I think they might have seen me."

It took all of Portia's self-control to not immediately look in the direction of the ale sellers. She knew if the Hares found them there, bad things would happen. The Hares did not look kindly on members of rival gangs poaching coppers in their district. Her heart pounded wildly as she moved her purse to a hidden spot within her tunic, hiding her motions from the crowd by facing Mark. She pulled out a second purse from her pants pocket, one constructed of cheap material, and draped its strap across her body. She reached down and grabbed a handful of pebbles and deposited them in the purse, giving it a weight that implied coins within. Dusting herself off, she tried to act casual and turned to walk down the lane, motioning with her fingertips for Mark to follow. He swallowed, then quickly stepped behind her as she walked down the street.

They made it to the far corner of the market, near the street that ran along the harbor towards the fishing warehouses. Portia breathed in deeply, thinking they had made it safely away from the Hares, when three boys, all wearing small green patches on their shirts, jumped out in front of them. The lead boy stepped in front of Portia, stopping her. The other two came in close as well, keeping an eye on Mark, who was shifting nervously from foot to foot behind her.

"No Cats here," the lead boy said, leaning in to Portia's face so closely that she smelled fish on his breath. He flipped his hair out of his eyes. The Hares all prided themselves on being fashionable, right down to the curls they all had falling in front of their eyes. Of all the orphan gangs in the city, they could afford it most of all. They controlled the harbor market, which was the richest market in all of Valencia.

"I don't know what you're talking about," Portia said as she tried to step around the boy. He leered at her, knowing she was lying. Portia glanced around, trying to spy something to use as a distraction to get away from the boys blocking their path. He stepped even closer and grabbed her upper arms. Mark gasped from behind her.

"We're not joking here. No Black Cats. Got it?" He gave her a little shake and tried to tower over her even further, which was not that effective considering how tall she was for her age of nearly thirteen years. He only had an inch on her.

She took a deep breath, and on exhale she swiftly brought both arms up between his and swung them up and out, breaking his grip. When his arms went wide, she noticed an envelope in the inside pocket of his jacket. Perhaps it was something important to gang business. If she could get the letter, and get away with it, maybe Deyelna would take it easy on them when they returned. As leader of the Black Cats, her wrath was nearly as intimidating as being caught by the Hares.

Portia stepped back, bumping into Mark. He faced the two other Hares, who were trying to grab him just as the lead had grabbed Portia. He held a small knife out, swiping at their grasping hands every time one of the boys got close. Over Mark's head, Portia noticed a wagon coming from the market with bales of hay hanging off its bed. The horses were pulling the wagon on a course that would pass right by them. She elbowed Mark and gave a small nod towards the wagon. His eyes flickered in acknowledgment. She and Mark kept circling, dodging and knocking away the other boys' grasping hands, until the wagon was just next to them. Portia leapt up towards the wagon, grabbed the bale of hay closest to them, and pulled it sharply towards herself. It toppled off the wagon and broke its binding, scattering into a large pile of loose straw, getting the attention of the driver. He yelled sharply and pulled up the reins, stopping the horses short, and turned his attention to the kids. He jumped off the wagon and strode towards them, brandishing his whip as a weapon.

As soon as Portia saw the lead boy's head turn towards the wagon driver, she leapt forward towards him, stuck her hand into his jacket, and grabbed the letter. She gripped it tightly and pulled it in towards herself while the boy reacted by grabbing her bag strap at the same time. She jerked back quickly, and her strap broke as he hung on to it. She grabbed Mark by the arm and pulled him around the back of the wagon to the harbor side. They ran towards the fish warehouses. The Hares scattered in a different direction, leaving the angry wagon driver swinging his whip in frustration at the mess beside his wagon.

Portia and Mark rounded the corner of the nearest warehouse, out of sight of the market. Portia leaned over, breathing heavily. Mark slumped against the wall of the warehouse, trying to catch his breath.

Portia turned to Mark. "Why did you pull your knife? One of those kids could have grabbed it from you. The guards usually turn a blind eye to us, but they won't if you stab someone."

"I didn't stab anyone. It was just to get us some space," Mark muttered.

Portia stared at Mark. She didn't want to push him too far. It had been hard for him since he lost his parents. He'd been with Portia since he was five years old, when she had found him alone on the streets of Valencia one evening, dirty and hungry. Since that time, she'd felt responsible for him. Portia was the one that talked John into letting Mark join the gang. She wanted him safe. "At least we got away," she said. "How much did you get by the pastry stall?"

Mark reached for his purse but ended up grasping only empty space. He turned, banging his head slowly against the wall.

"Hey, they didn't get everything, did they?" Portia asked. "Please tell me they didn't?"

"No, I'm not an idiot," Mark said, red-faced. He reached into his tunic, pulled out a small leather bag. He opened it, poured its contents into one hand. He counted it with one finger. "Twenty coppers."

Portia's stomach knotted. "We need thirty each—"

"I know. I know..." Mark said. He turned away from her.

Deyelna was looking for any excuse to kick them out of the Black Cats. They had to pay their dues today, no excuses. The extreme difficulty of pickpocketing enough coppers in the farmers' market, the Black Cat's territory, was why they had risked going to the harbor market today. The merchants and their customers always seemed to have more coin on them than the farmers and their customers.

Mark kicked at the ground, his face screwed up. He wiped at his eyes, pretending he was angry and not crying. Portia checked her own purse. She found forty coppers in it.

"Don't worry," she said, handing over ten coppers to Mark. "We've got enough. Let's head back."

Mark nodded and took the coins from Portia without looking at her. They walked quietly for a few moments. Portia snuck a glance at Mark and saw that he still looked down at his feet. She jokingly pushed his upper arm. He ignored her. She pushed harder, almost knocking him over. He laughed and finally looked up. He wiped his nose as they walked towards the Black Cat territory.

They reached the farmers' market and found it just as crowded as the harbor market. Portia looked around. There were enough customers that day that she considered whether they should continue working there to make up for what they lost to the Hares. She thought she saw someone dressed in black duck away into a leather shop when she had turned to look, but decided she was feeling paranoid from their earlier encounter. She motioned to Mark that they should go to a bakery stall to continue working. Once there, she turned to scan the crowd again and this time caught sight of a figure, clothed entirely in black, once again ducking into a shop when she looked. The hairs on the back of her neck stood up.

"Someone is following us. Did you notice anyone in all black at the harbor market?" Portia asked Mark as she pretended to examine loaves of bread in a bin.

"I only noticed the Hares. Is it one of them?" Mark asked.

"I don't think so," Portia answered. "This person seems older somehow. But I can't get a good look at their face."

Mark swallowed. "I wonder if it's an enforcer from the harbor market."

"You think they would've stopped us by now if they had a reason to," Portia said, "unless they don't want anyone to see what they are doing." Portia didn't want to know what sort of bad things a person might want to do when no one else could see. Especially if it was to her and Mark.

She looked again in the direction she had last seen the figure in black and noticed the person was much nearer, walking closely behind a loaded farmer's wagon coming their way. Frustratingly, she still couldn't get a good look at the pursuer's face. But they were close enough that she could see the figure's broad shoulders. It must be a man.

Mark turned and saw who she was looking at. His face tensed as he whirled, scanning the market for a hiding spot.

Portia didn't want to get trapped in the market. Instead, she nudged Mark in the direction of the alleyway behind the bakery stall. They bolted down the dark, dirty opening between the buildings, weaving between abandoned crates and piles of garbage. Portia heard loud footfalls behind her and the crash of crates being knocked over. The man in black was fast—and had given up all pretense of stealth.

Bursting out of the alley, Portia and Mark led their pursuer down a side street past the tailors, towards another alley. Portia wanted to draw the pursuer away from the market and then lose him. She knew of just the place to do that, if they could keep from being caught before they got there. She pushed another burst of speed, even though her legs were burning with the effort.

Reaching another alley, Portia took a sharp right into it, grabbing Mark and pulling him with her. They ran to the end where there was a small fence spanning from side to side, blocking the passage.

"No good!" Mark said.

"Go!" Portia said, not letting go of Mark. She shoved him towards a small gap on the right between the fence and the brick building. He turned sideways and squeezed through. Portia slid behind him. She was slowed down by the tight fit, wiggling to get past the fence. Mark turned and noticed her struggle. He grabbed her hand and yanked her through.

It had been a long time since she'd used that route to escape the guards. She'd been clumsy when she had first learned how to pickpocket and once or twice had a victim yell out for the authorities. The guards had chased her pell-mell through the streets of Valencia. It'd been close a few times, but she'd always managed to lose them using this fence. But it looked like she'd have to devise another escape trick soon in case it was ever needed because she was growing too large to pass through the gap.

The pursuer slammed into the wooden fence as Portia and Mark backed away from it. The man on the other side slammed into it again and again. The fence moved with each impact, but the old wood held. Portia and Mark ran away from the shuddering barrier as quietly as they could.

Several blocks away, when it was clear they had lost

their pursuer, they stopped to catch their breath. Portia pulled off her jacket, flipped it inside out, and put it back on, revealing a now maroon exterior and hiding the black she had originally worn on the outside. "I don't know who that was, but I don't want to run into him again," Portia said, as she pulled out a thin cotton cap from her bag and tucked her hair inside it. "Come on, we still need to get some money for food."

"Where?" Mark asked. "Back at the farmers' market? What if we run into that guy again?"

Portia hesitated, but decided she couldn't let fear rule her. "We have to eat. He probably has no idea we're normally there," Portia said.

"We have no idea who he is... or why he chased us," Mark said.

"It was probably just by chance," Portia said, while feeling in her heart that was not the case. But they had to make money and could not just go home. And she was pretty sure they had led the man far enough away from the market that he wouldn't think to return there to look for them again. At least she hoped so. Her stomach growled, making the task more urgent. She hadn't had any breakfast that day. They didn't have a single extra copper on them to buy food. "I'm not worried. I want to keep working," she said as she straightened up, shaking her shoulders.

Mark shook his head no. "Not me. I've had enough for today."

Portia wanted to argue but knew better. It would be quicker and easier if she went alone. Mark did not have the touch for thieving. "Suit yourself. See you back at the house," Portia said. "Be careful."

Mark nodded. He watched her walk off and turned to the direction of the Black Cats' house.

When Portia arrived at the farmers' market, she noticed a familiar female guard in the patrol working the market. That guard had been patrolling the farmers' market for as long as Portia could remember. There were not that many women guards, at least not that she'd seen from her explorations in the city. This particular one didn't tolerate nonsense from anybody. Portia liked her.

Portia looked around the market, trying to decide where to start. Lunchtime had come and gone, and the crowd of customers was thinning as the day drew nearer to market closing time. She decided to work near the produce sellers who were discounting their wares, rather than having to drag them back home. These discounts were drawing enough people that Portia thought she could work unnoticed.

She first lifted a copper from a young man in blue who was preoccupied trying to impress a young woman he fancied. While he was leaning forward to select the best apple, Portia bumped into him while pretending to cough. He backed away in concern from her, fearing her ill, which worked as planned to distract him from her hand digging in his purse. She mumbled an apology under her breath to him and quickly backed away. He glared at her, then slowly turned his attention back to his sweetheart. She repeated this process several times, managing to grab at least one coin each time.

Her luck ran out, however, when she tried to get a copper

from a harried matron who had the wrist of a screaming child in each hand. The matron felt her touch and whirled on her, already red-faced from screaming at her children. "What are you all about!" she demanded.

"Nothing. Sorry, ma'am," Portia said, backing up.

"I saw you, girl! You were digging in her purse," an apple seller yelled at Portia. "That girl's a thief! Guards! Guards!"

Portia saw the apple seller pointing at her. She bolted down the aisle between stalls. She could hear the yells of the matron and the apple seller behind her, pointing her out to the guards. She weaved between people, trying to figure out a place to hide. Abruptly, a guard stepped out in front of her—it was the female guard she had noticed before—and Portia veered to the left to avoid her.

Portia ran past behind the butcher's stall, the guard chasing after her. Portia gained some time by being able to quickly duck between people, leaving the larger guard to have to brute force push through the crowds. Fumbling with her purse, Portia dropped a few coins in the path of the guard, then dove under the skirting of a table in the back of the nearby fabric tent. She peeked out underneath it to see if she was followed. She saw the guard slow near where she had dropped the coins. The woman leaned over, pretended to catch her breath, while stealthily picking up the coppers that Portia had dropped. Portia saw the guard slyly pocket the coppers, then she turned towards the apple seller and told her she did not know where the thief had gone, while still pretending to be out of breath.

Portia pulled back from the skirting and breathed a sigh of

relief. She leaned back against the wall the table was up against and pulled out her purse to count her earnings. When she grabbed the purse, her fingers felt the envelope she had stolen earlier from the Hare boy. She had forgotten about it.

Pulling out the letter, she examined the envelope. A thick green wax seal held it closed. She recognized the symbol of the Hares pressed within it. There was no name or any other writing on the outside, and she felt no magic from it prohibiting others than the intended person from reading it. Portia exhaled sharply. There was only one way to find out what was within. She broke through the thick wax and opened the letter.

The letter was addressed to the Serpents, another rival orphan gang. Luckily, the letter was printed and not written in script—something that she could not read. John had said he was going to teach her the flowing loops of the ancient way of writing, but he died before that was possible. The letter listed a time and location of a meeting between the Hares and the Black Cats. The only other words were "Crash as planned," which were scrawled in a messy hand. *Crash what?* Portia wondered. Why would the Hares send a letter with details of their own private meeting to a rival gang? And why didn't she know of the planned meeting between the Hares and the Black Cats? What was Deyelna up to? It didn't make sense to Portia. Perhaps the boy who had confronted her was a spy within his own gang. But that letter was visible to the two other boys he was with, and surely a real spy would not be that bold, even with his own gang.

Portia held the letter in her hands, gently tapping it to her forehead to try to understand what was going on. She noticed a clerk reach under the other end of the table to retrieve a box. Luckily, the man did not see Portia. This was not a safe place to linger. Giving up on figuring out the letter, she folded it back up and stashed it within her jacket. She counted her coins—thirty-four coppers. It was enough for her dues and some food, but she didn't dare buy anything at the market with the apple seller looking for her. She sighed heavily and decided to head back to the Black Cats' house.

Portia waited until the fabric clerk was distracted with the customer and then crawled out from under the table. Walking through the market quickly, she noticed the sun was nearly set. This was bad. To reach the Black Cats' house, she would have to pass near the warehouses that were now controlled by the Serpents. The Serpents were a gang that was well known for backstabbing and physical violence. Their ruthless tactics had been effective in encroaching on what had formerly been Black Cat territory. There was no way to avoid going near their area, however, without encircling the entire city, because of the nearby Smithing district where the Lynxes were in control, a gang who were equally brutal. The Black Cat territory was being pinched between the two rival gangs. If things continued, they would lose control of the farmers' market because it would be too dangerous to get there.

Portia walked along the now darkening street. She tried to keep to the long strips of sun still left, avoiding the shadows. There were few people out. Anyone who was smart was getting inside before the sun set. She picked her way along, avoiding the trash that littered the way. A rat scurried out in her path. She jumped a bit but managed not to scream. She picked up her pace, looking left and right to make sure she didn't see any other orphans.

Turning a corner, she nearly ran into a man who was thrust into the street from a nearby tavern. He was followed out by two rough-looking men. One of the men grabbed the victim by the collar and punched him right in front of Portia. Her eyes widened. She took off running. She did not want their ire to fall on her. One of the men yelled out to grab her because she was a witness, but the other said to let her go because she was just a kid. Portia kept running in case he changed his mind. She knew many an adult had died on that street. Someday, she would live in a place where she didn't have to risk death every day.

Finally, she passed into the Black Cat neighborhood. The sturdier construction of the warehouse district gave way to old wooden homes, and even some shacks, once meant to be temporary but still in use many years later. The house where the Black Cats lived was over one hundred years old, drafty, and creaky. But it was home.

Portia walked up to the blue-stained front door. She knocked an intricate pattern. A single knock answered her from within. She mumbled "Night sky," that day's password. The door opened slowly, and she saw two Peters—or at least one Peter and one image of him. Peter was an older enforcer for the Black Cats. He was nearing the age of majority and was the second or third in command behind Deyelna. His magical ability was to create a duplicate of himself.

Portia was annoyed that he was using it on her. She sighed

heavily. "Why are you watching the door instead of Jack? You hate door duty."

Peter shrugged his shoulders. "I'm waiting for you, and I could watch the door at the same time. This way, I could send Jack to get me some dinner." Peter smirked in his own cleverness. If he was anything, it was efficient. He backed up to give Portia room to enter.

Portia stepped in and the Peter to her right disappeared. She cursed at herself for not being able to figure out which Peter was the real one. She couldn't tell where his voice had come from. Did he learn to throw his voice too? Or was that part of the magic? She needed to find that out.

"Mark has paid his dues," Peter said. "Deyelna is waiting for you to come pay yours. I'll take you to her." Peter stood with his arms crossed, making it clear he expected Portia to follow him immediately.

Portia's stomach tightened. "Can't I just give you the coins?" Portia asked. She didn't usually have to see Deyelna to pay her dues. There must be another reason. Knowing Deyelna, it would not be a pleasant one for Portia. Deyelna hated Portia from the first day they met, well before Deyelna was the leader of the Black Cats. It had only become worse since John, the previous Black Cat leader, had died. Deyelna had taken over as head Black Cat. Since then, it had been a constant struggle for Portia to not be evicted from the gang. Deyelna looked for any excuse to get rid of her. The only thing that had saved Portia so far was the rules that John had put in place about gang behavior and the possibility of revolt if

Deyelna arbitrarily pushed Portia out without following those rules.

Peter shook his head no. "Sorry, plebe, the leader calls, and when the leader calls, you come running." Peter tapped his foot impatiently. "Get a move on, you're keeping me from Merticle's *Second Volume of History*. He's about to tell how the Karaths took over the world in the second century."

Portia knew there was no getting out of this. Peter would enforce anything Deyelna wanted. She might as well get it over with. She nodded at Peter, straightening her shoulders to face what was next.

Peter turned and walked deeper into the house. Portia followed. Peter flicked his fingers at a Black Cat member sitting in the dark living room they passed on their way to the back of the house. The member rose and walked to the seat used when guarding the front door. Peter didn't even turn his head to make sure his order was followed. Portia could not remember a time when someone had disobeyed Peter.

They walked deeper into the dark house towards Deyelna's lair.

2

Peter abruptly stopped in an open doorway. Portia barely stopped herself before walking into him. He looked in the room and nodded to its occupant, Merwin, a Black Cat member who was lounging in a chair with his feet on the desk, keeping an eye on the doorway. Merwin survived in the gang by being the local bookie. Portia had never seen him out pickpocketing. Instead, he favored the horse racetrack on the edge of town. He usually took bets from members of other gangs, but occasionally he would take one or two from the Black Cats members. But he purposefully didn't take too many—it got to be awkward if too many Black Cats lost at once.

"Hey," Peter said. "Those races were a mess today."

Merwin nodded back at Peter. "Those races, or your choices?"

"I had a sure thing. Based on all the races I've seen before, Fire Storm should have won," Peter said glumly. "I was counting on those winnings."

"That is not a good idea. But I think you know that now," Merwin said with a twinkle in his eye. He had some sympathies for his clients, but he wasn't above teasing them. He didn't take anything too seriously.

Portia crossed her arms and stared at Peter. She wanted to go rest. She couldn't do that until after she paid her dues. "I thought Deyelna wanted to see me."

Peter turned to Portia, irritation on his face. "This won't take long. I'm surprised you're in such a rush." He pointedly looked at her crossed arms. Portia uncrossed them and tried to banish the irritation from her face. She wondered what Peter's comment on her impatience meant. Did Peter know something that he wasn't sharing about her upcoming meeting with Deyelna? It didn't matter. Whatever it was wasn't going to get any better by waiting. She might as well find out what Deyelna wanted.

Peter pulled out his coin bag, counted out a few coins, and handed them to Merwin. Portia tried to see how much he was paying, but Peter kept his back between her and his outstretched hand, purposely blocking her vision. He snorted at her attempt to be nosy. "Let's go," he said as he turned away from the doorway and led her further into the house. Portia saw Merwin tuck a coin into his dreads for good luck as they walked away.

Portia followed Peter. Looking down the hall in the direction that she and Peter were walking, she saw Mark come out of the kitchen. He nodded at her. As they passed Mark, Portia grabbed his arm. "Did you pay your dues?" she asked.

"Yes," Mark said, glancing at Peter who was watching

their exchange. "Had to pay them right to the boss this month. She was pretty pissed."

"About your dues?" Portia asked.

"No, but something was bugging her." Mark said. Portia knew Mark was just as uncomfortable with Deyelna as she was, but he was smart enough not to say too much in front of Peter. She'd have to talk to him about it later.

"You going to see her now?" Mark asked.

"Yes, she is," Peter answered for her, motioning for Mark to continue down the hallway. "Off now."

Mark grimaced at Peter's dismissal, but he merely nodded, then walked off. Portia was glad he didn't get into it with Peter. A fight with Deyelna's favorite enforcer was the last thing they needed right now.

Peter and Portia walked past the kitchen and finally reached the painted-over French doors that separated Deyelna's domain from the rest of the house. Peter knocked three quick knocks, paused, then knocked another three quick raps. Portia heard a silky voice from within say to come in. Peter opened the door and gestured for Portia to enter.

Portia entered Deyelna's room. Deyelna was sprawled on a large green velvet chair that faced the doorway, one of her legs draped over the overstuffed arm. Deyelna's dark eyes were trained on a Black Cat member who was perched on the edge of a wooden chair in front of her. She smoothed a section of her long black hair over and over again while the Black Cat member in front of her studied the floor. Finally, Deyelna looked up at Portia, considered her for a second, then waved her fingers in dismissal to the Black Cat. The gang member quickly got off the chair and scurried around Portia and out of the room. Portia heard the door click behind her.

Deyelna did not say anything to Portia. The silence hung in the room.

Portia swallowed, then said, "I'm here to pay my dues."

Deyelna nodded, gestured to a strongbox on a table along the wall. "You can put it in there. I *trust* you to put in the right amount." Portia knew Deyelna was really telling her she didn't trust her. There was an edge of anger to Deyelna's voice that was different from her normal standard dislike of Portia.

Portia walked over to the strongbox and lifted the lid.

"Is there anything you want to mention while you're here?" Deyelna asked from behind her.

Portia's hands froze for a second. She forced herself to keep counting her coins, mentally willing her hands to stop shaking. "No, nothing," she replied. Portia heard the quiver in her voice and hoped Deyelna did not notice. She dropped her thirty coppers into the strongbox and shut it. She forced her face to relax then turned to face Deyelna.

Deyelna glared at her. This was not the answer she had wanted to hear. She brought her leg down off the chair arm and leaned in towards Portia, a look of concentration on her face.

Portia knew that Deyelna was trying to use her glam magic on her. Deyelna had a strong magical ability to make people do what she wanted them to do. It was a formidable magical skill to have. She could feel the pressure on her brain as Deyelna tried to enforce her will upon Portia. Few people could resist it, or even notice it as it was worked upon them.

Portia didn't know of anyone in the Black Cats who could resist it now, except her. John had been able to, but he was long gone. She had avoided bringing her ability to withstand Deyelna's magic to the leader's attention because it only enraged her. But this time she would have no choice but to point-blank fight it.

Deyelna tried harder, sending shoots of pain through Portia's head. Portia winced in response. She clenched her jaws shut. Deyelna was trying to make her talk. Portia strengthened her resolve to not give in to Deyelna's pressure.

Portia knew that somehow Deyelna could tell her magic was not working on Portia. She had tried in the past to act slightly dazed and pretend that it was, but somehow Deyelna always knew. The rage on Deyelna's face had terrified Portia the first time it had happened—her eyes had bulged, and she had raised fists to strike Portia. Luckily, John had been there to stop her.

She was on her own this time. She held on, hoping Deyelna would give up before she passed out from the agony in her head.

Deyelna exhaled in frustration. She stopped trying her magic on Portia. Portia breathed a sigh of relief as the pain left her head.

Standing abruptly, Deyelna paced in front of her throne chair. "You were always a problem, Portia," Deyelna said. "Why are you making it worse by going into the Hare's territory?"

Portia did not respond.

Deyelna stopped pacing. She stared at Portia. "I'll take

that as a confirmation." She squinted her eyes at Portia, rage filling them. "The rules are clear, *member*. As a Black Cat, you work in the Black Cat territory. This is how it works."

Deyelna walked directly in front of Portia. She crossed her arms and breathed into Portia's face. "Do you understand? I don't even know why I'm asking you, because clearly you don't, or you *won't*, understand this."

Portia tried to not inhale Deyelna's breath. "I understand the rules... but we can't make enough money in the farmers' market to pay our dues."

"Yet everyone else manages to," Deyelna replied.

Portia longed to ask if she was really sure about that. She had seen other members sneak off once or twice to try different areas, but she wasn't a snitch. It wasn't her place to tell Deyelna what the members of her gang were doing.

"We're trying... I'm trying. But if I can't get enough money, what else am I supposed to do?" Portia asked.

"Improve your thieving skills, *member*," Deyelna replied. "John always said you are a talented thief. What happened?"

Portia stiffened at the insult to her abilities. She *was* a good thief. It was just harder now. The crops had failed just as the kingdom had raised taxes. "The people are suffering these days. They don't have as much coin as they used to—and they watch their purses all the more carefully because of that," Portia said. Didn't Deyelna ever go on the streets anymore? How could she not know what was happening in Valencia?

"Then you'll have to be more skilled, won't you?" Deyelna said. She stepped back from Portia and walked back to her throne. She fell back into it, once more sprawling out.

"Besides, I have a plan. I'm going to take care of this issue. There is more going on than *you* would know about, *member*," Deyelna said, her voice thick with contempt. "I'm the leader here, understood? Your job is to do what you're told."

Portia bristled at Deyelna's attitude, but she shoved her anger back down. Now was not the time to push back. She wondered if Deyelna's plan had anything to do with the meeting mentioned in the letter. If Deyelna was going to be at that meeting between the Hares and the Black Cats, she probably had no idea about the Hares instructing the Serpents to crash it. It must be a trap set by the Hares. The thought of Deyelna taking the fall mollified Portia somewhat.

But would she and Mark be safer if Deyelna lost power?

Portia shook her head. No. Deyelna might be a bully, but she knew how to deal with her. Portia herself was too young to lead the Black Cats, nor did she want to. She also didn't know what would happen if someone found out she had knowledge to protect Deyelna and failed to do so. "Does it have anything to do with the Hares?" Portia asked.

Deyelna narrowed her eyes at Portia. "Why would you ask that?"

Portia swallowed. "I think the Hares are setting a trap for you," she blurted out.

"And how would you know that?" Deyelna squinted at Portia. "And why would I believe you?" Deyelna tapped her fingers on the arm of her chair. "Is this why you have been going into Hare territory? To set up a traitorous plot?"

"No! I was just trying to make some money. We were attacked by the Hares." Portia hesitated. She wanted to show

Deyelna proof that she was loyal to the Black Cats. Maybe that would get her off her back. Or maybe it would further infuriate her leader. She looked at Deyelna sprawled on her chair, and indignation at being berated by her overtook Portia. "I stole this letter in the fight." Portia pulled out the letter and thrust it out to Deyelna.

Deyelna looked at the letter and then up at Portia's face. "What is this?" She was not in a hurry to touch it.

Portia shook the letter. "It's from the Hares to the Serpents."

Deyelna looked at her skeptically.

"It's about... your meeting with them," Portia insisted.

"I don't believe you," Deyelna said, but she took the letter from Portia's hand. She examined the seal on the outside then quickly scanned its contents. She folded it back up and slammed it on the table in front of her. "This is a fake. Who gave this to you? Or did you come up with it yourself?"

Portia could feel the anger radiating off Deyelna. Surely Deyelna didn't think she would betray her?

"I... couldn't come up with that. How would I even know about your meeting?" Portia asked.

"I don't know—yet. But you're sneaky. I don't put it past you."

"I grabbed it out of the jacket of a Hare. He didn't want me to have it," Portia protested.

"And what did this *Hare* look like?" Deyelna asked, skeptically.

Portia racked her brain to try to remember. Everything

had happened so fast. "He was just a little taller than me and had dark curly hair—"

"They all have dark curly hair," Deyelna said, waving her arm in frustration. "You aren't telling me anything helpful. I don't understand why you think I should believe you."

"Because you're the leader of our gang," Portia said. "Why would I betray you?"

Deyelna stared over Portia's right shoulder, considering her options while still drumming her fingers on her chair arm. She finally turned to Portia. "I need proof. I need proof this letter is real. *You* and Mark are going to go to the Serpents' territory and get it for me."

Portia's stomach tightened. Poaching from the Hares was one thing, but messing with the Serpents was another thing entirely. They were not a gang to be taken lightly. They were violent. And not afraid of bloodshed. Thieving was the least of their crimes. The thought of having to face them, or getting caught in their territory terrified her. Furthermore, she couldn't bear the thought of Mark being in danger with her. "They might not even know about this yet. Not if I took the letter," Portia protested.

Deyelna picked up the letter and glanced inside. "It says *crash as planned.* If this letter is real, someone there will know about this. And since you're the one telling me about this, it makes the most sense that you should go and prove it."

"At least leave Mark out of this. I'll go on my own," Portia said.

"No. Mark goes with you."

"Why? He has nothing to do with this," Portia said. She

could hear the anxiety in her voice and cursed herself for not controlling her emotions better. Deyelna would insist even more if she knew how much Portia feared for Mark.

"Because I said so," Deyelna said. "I'm the leader here, and I'm tired of your back talk. Either you and Mark do this, or you're both evicted from the gang."

A pain shot through Portia's heart. The gang was the only family she had known. Losing it would be the end of her world. She knew Deyelna couldn't stand her, but to force her and Mark onto the street so casually was a level of betrayal that took her breath away. Deyelna must be confident in her ability to control the rest of the gang after such an action.

"Fine," Portia said, trying to keep her voice steady. "We'll do it. But I'm going to protect Mark and keep him out of trouble."

"Whatever," Deyelna said. "Just as long as you get it done." She waved her dismissal at Portia.

Portia turned and exited Deyelna's lair. She made her way back to the room she shared with Mark. Opening the door, she saw him on the pile of old blankets that was his makeshift bed on the floor. She sighed, turned to her own bed, and pulled off her purse and knife belt. She dreaded telling Mark what Deyelna had said.

"Did you find out why she's pissed?" Mark asked.

"Not really. She knows about us going into the Hares' territory."

"Ugh." Mark said. "You said she wouldn't know."

"I don't know how she knew it," Portia said. "But..." She

turned to Mark. "It gets worse. She wants us to go to the Serpents' territory."

Mark looked at her questioningly. Portia explained about the letter and what it said about the meeting. She told him about Deyelna's threat to evict them. He turned pale as she told him.

"Peter's told me about the Serpents. They hate the Black Cats," Mark said, looking ill. "They caught a Black Cat in their territory a few years ago when Peter had just joined the gang. They kept the Black Cat prisoner for a week. When they finally released him, he came back to the gang but never spoke another word again. Not one. They took his tongue."

"That's just a story Peter said to scare you," Portia said.

"No. That's what they do to spies," Mark said. "It's a message. They cut their tongues out so they can't speak."

"Even if it's true that they captured someone, he probably didn't talk because he was scared of them," Portia said, putting a brave face on it. She refused to believe that it was true that a gang would mutilate someone like that. She couldn't believe it was true because they had to go deal with them. If the Serpents were that vicious, she would lose her nerve. "It doesn't matter anyway, because if we don't do what Deyelna says, she'll kick us out of the gang. We'll be on the streets without protection."

"The Serpents truly don't like spies. I think they really did it."

Portia didn't answer Mark. She sat down heavily on her bed, putting her head in her hands. "We have to go and find one of them that knows about this meeting. Or get proof, somehow, that they are in league with the Hares."

"Can't we just grab one of the Hares and make them talk? They are less scary," Mark said, the edge of a plea in his voice.

"No, Deyelna was clear."

Portia did wonder why they couldn't prove it with one of the Hares. She considered going back and making that case to Deyelna, but she knew that risked enraging Deyelna even further. Their leader was known for doing rash things when in the throes of a rage. She could see them getting immediately banished if she pushed too hard.

"It's probably a trap," Mark said quietly.

Portia looked up. She knew Mark more than likely was right, but what could they do?

"Well, let's not get caught," Portia said. She shook herself slightly. This was not the time to get morose or let Peter's tales get to her.

"Okay. We might as well get this over with before Deyelna comes up with something worse," Mark said, getting up. He gathered up his own knife belt and purse from underneath his pillow and put them on.

"Have you eaten?" Portia asked. Her own stomach was growling since she hadn't been able to buy anything at the market.

"Yeah, I did," Mark said. He pulled out a half roll and cheese and handed it to Portia. She looked at him questioningly. He shrugged. "I nicked it from the cook."

"Like we aren't in enough trouble," Portia said.

Mark looked at her mischievously. "I think Cook lets me get away with it."

Portia wasn't going to argue with Mark. Cook probably did let him get away with it. She had no idea why the cantankerous old woman favored Mark over the rest of them, but at this moment she was grateful. She shoved the sandwich into her mouth and chewed quickly while she gathered her own thieving tools: a set of lockpicks, some thin but strong rope, and a few caltrops. She stashed these tools in a small bag she wore under her jacket, preparing herself for the huge challenge ahead.

When she was finished, she turned and nodded at Mark. He nodded back. Together they walked out of the safety of their room.

3

P ortia and Mark exited the Black Cat's house and stepped into the dark street. Portia hoped they would have better luck escaping notice under the cover of night. They turned in the direction of the warehouse district and walked down the nearly deserted street. They had about half a mile to go, so Portia thought this would be a good time to refresh Mark on her rules—the rules she had come up with years ago to protect herself when thieving. Those rules would probably help them in spying.

"Remember the rules," Portia said.

Mark looked at her, then rolled his eyes. "I know the rules."

"Just in case, let's go over them... One: don't be the attacker—"

"Always defend yourself against attack," Mark interrupted. He continued on in a singsong voice, "Two: don't draw attention to yourself. Always walk normally, like you aren't sneaking." He skipped, doing a little dance to his words, wiggling his butt and making Portia laugh despite herself. "Three: have a backup plan—never go into a place you don't know how to get out of. Four," he pointed at Portia, waving his index finger at her, "go in at the highest point of the building because it's less likely someone will question you. And finally, five: slow people down so they can't fight you." He stopped dancing at the end of his recitation and gave her a little bow.

Portia sighed. "As long as you know them." She looked meaningfully at him. "Especially the part about not fighting."

Mark did not acknowledge her words. He turned once again towards the warehouses and walked determinedly. Portia sighed once again and fell in alongside him.

The residential houses thinned until there were just one or two per block separated by junkyards and decrepit businesses. Finally, the houses disappeared once and for all, leaving a desolate block of open space before the looming warehouses ahead of them. The shadows between the warehouses were pitch-black, not even receiving a sliver of moonlight.

Portia and Mark looked for observers but saw no one besides a wagon caravan coming from the city behind them, and Portia motioned for Mark to step back. They waited for the caravan to approach. When it passed them, Portia and Mark fell in line behind the last wagon as if they were part of it. This way, they crossed the open space before the warehouses started, hopefully not attracting any special notice.

Once they were between two warehouses, Portia motioned to Mark to climb a narrow metal ladder attached to one of the buildings. The ladder led up to the roof. Mark jumped up, grabbed the bottom rung which hung five feet off the street, and pulled himself up. He climbed three rungs before the metal ladder gave a loud groan. Mark stopped climbing immediately. Both he and Portia looked around. No one seemed to have noticed. There was no cry of alarm. No running footsteps. Mark gingerly started climbing again. Portia waited a second then leapt up to the bottom rung and followed him to the roof.

Mark and Portia walked along the edge of the warehouse roof. They looked for a Serpent wandering the streets below. When they got to the far side of the building, Mark spied someone and pointed out a dark, skulking figure in the alleyway below to Portia. They watched as the figure walked carefully down the dark alley, keeping close to the wall as if trying to avoid notice. They followed along on the roof in the direction the figure was walking. The figure hurried its pace until Mark and Portia were running on the rooftop to keep up. They were stopped by a massive looming wall ahead of them —it was the exterior wall of the next adjacent warehouse. It rose ten feet higher than the building they currently stood on. They'd have to find a way onto its roof, and quickly, if they wanted to keep following the figure. Unfortunately, there was no nearby ladder, and the figure below disappeared around the corner of the next block before they found a way up. Mark sighed in frustration.

"This warehouse seems to be the highest around," Mark said, pointing to the warehouse in front of them. "Perhaps we should check inside here first."

"Agreed. First, let's get on top."

Portia and Mark ran quietly along the wall of the warehouse until they reached another metal ladder that led up to the roof of the higher structure. They climbed it. When they reached the top, they could see unobstructed in every direction. No nearby building was higher than the one they were standing on. They were safe from being spied on as long as they carefully stood back a few feet from the building's sides, so that no one could look up from the street and see them.

They walked along the side of the building, carefully keeping a few feet back, and looked for the spill of light on the street below that would give away the location of a window in the warehouse above it. Hopefully, the lights would be on in the building—otherwise they would have to come up with another plan. But they were in luck. Portia spied a window shaped puddle of yellow light in the alleyway fifty feet ahead. She pointed it out to Mark. They ran to the corresponding location on the roof.

Mark carefully walked to the edge, got on his stomach, and leaned over. Portia sat on his legs, keeping him from falling over as he edged his head and upper chest out to see in the window. He looked for a few minutes then twitched his right leg twice, signaling to Portia to help pull him back up.

Once up, he sat heavily, his face beet red from hanging upside down. He shook his head rapidly to clear the blood. "It was hard to see, but it looks like an office. I could see through a window in the office door that the warehouse was full of goods, except for an opening in the middle of the boxes." He looked at her meaningful. "It would be the perfect place for secret gang meetings. Especially if the owner didn't know about it."

Portia nodded. She pulled out her rope. She tried to remember which one of them was heavier—they had both grown so much, so quickly, in the last few years. He was definitely thinner. But even if he was lighter, she didn't want him risking going into the warehouse first. She felt responsible for him. She looked around the roof for anything they could use as an anchor. There was a small brick chimney. She kicked at it and not a brick moved. It was solid. Portia wrapped the rope around it several times and then handed the end to Mark. He would be the last stop if the chimney didn't hold. She hoped it would not come to that. The last thing she wanted was both of them in a broken heap on the street below.

"Knot this around your waist and lean back until I get inside. I'll look for a spot to tie up so you can follow," Portia said as she handed the rope to Mark.

Mark nodded in agreement. He tied the rope around his waist and handed the loose end to Portia. She tied it around herself and went over the edge of the building. Carefully holding the rope tight between her and the chimney, she leaned over slowly and then walked down along the building wall, letting out rope as she went.

She continued walking down on the vertical side of the building, her stomach in her mouth. She refused to look to the street below. She could do this because she had to, but heights were not her thing. She looked down only occasionally to make sure she was coming down above the window.

Portia's arms shook with the effort of letting out the rope.

She only had a few more feet of slack until she reached the knot around her waist. Luckily, it was enough, and she reached the window.

Portia gingerly put one foot on the narrow window ledge and then brought down her second foot. She crouched the best she could sideways, carefully freeing one hand, and pushed up on the window. It wouldn't budge. She peered inside. The lock on the window was not set—and why would it be? The window was several stories about street level. It must be stuck.

Shifting her position to get better leverage, she pushed up again. Still the window wouldn't move. Portia cursed under her breath and rested for a moment, clinging on the window edge.

"Are you okay?" Mark said softly from the roof.

Portia didn't want to answer for the noise it would make but was afraid Mark would come investigate is she didn't respond. "Yes," she said quietly. "The window is stuck. Hold on."

Portia reached inside her jacket for a small metal tool to use as a lever on the bottom of the window. Unfortunately, a caltrop came out along with the tool and dropped to the ground below. She silently cursed and held her breath until she heard the small tinkle of the caltrop hitting the hard-packed ground and then bouncing. Nothing reacted to the small noise. Portia exhaled then slipped the flat end of the metal tool under the bottom of the window. She pushed down and felt the window release. It must have been painted shut.

Portia slid open the window and lowered herself to the

floor within. Looking around, she saw she was in a tiny office with windows overlooking the warehouse area below. She untied the rope from around her waist and crab walked below the windows. She peered out but saw no one in the warehouse below. Unfortunately, there was nothing to tie a rope to in the office. They would have to leave this section tied to the chimney on the roof above. At least she knew it would hold Mark's weight.

She stuck her head outside and looked up. Mark looked down at her, concerned. Relief flooded her—she would not have to yell to get his attention. "Tie a good knot around the chimney and come down. Make sure to tie this end around yourself," she whispered, pushing her end of the rope back out the window. Mark nodded and pulled the rope up.

Her bag had one more section of rope. Good. She was not happy to have so little, but it was better than nothing. And hopefully they could get back up to the roof before the night was over and retrieve the larger piece now tied to the chimney. Strong, thin rope was expensive and hard to come by.

Mark lowered himself to the window and scrambled inside, crouching down to join her. He untied the rope. Portia shut the window quickly. The rope still hung from the roof but there was nothing they could do about that now. Hopefully no one would look up from the street and see it hanging.

"I don't think anyone saw me," Mark said. Portia nodded. "Are we going out that way?" Mark asked as he nodded at the office door.

"Yes. Wait here." Portia opened the door slowly and looked around. The office perched on a narrow catwalk that ran the length of the warehouse. The warehouse was a large open room except for the office on the catwalk. The huge space had a bare ceiling with exposed rafters. There were large doors on ground level on either end of the warehouse. Portia pulled her head back within the office and shut the door quietly. "We're going higher. There are rafters above that overlook everything."

Mark groaned but nodded back.

Portia once again opened the office door and exited, still crouched low. Mark followed. They scuttled to the end of the catwalk that was right below a rafter. Portia threw up the rope over the rafter and grabbed the end as it came over the far side. They quickly pulled themselves up to the rafter and withdrew the rope after themselves. Mark wobbled on his feet, sending Portia's heart into her mouth. "Be careful," she whispered.

He gave her a dark look. "No, I'm trying to fall to my death," he said sarcastically. Portia bit her tongue to not retort. He steadied himself and nodded back. He was ready to go.

They shuffled carefully along the rafters towards the far end of the warehouse where most of the goods were clustered. Portia could see the opening in the middle that Mark had mentioned. As they got closer, they heard voices drifting up from below. Portia looked to see where the lights were in the warehouse, wanting to make sure they did not come between the lights and the people below, alerting them to the intruders. Luckily, they were above the lights. They could pass on the rafters with the glare of the lights helping to hide them if anyone looked up.

They got close enough to where they could hear individual voices coming from within the opening in the goods. Portia did not want to go any further and risk being seen. Unfortunately, that meant not being able to see who was talking below. Portia motioned for Mark to stop and they crouched together, waiting for the voices to resolve into recognizable sentences.

"... it's good money," an older voice said from below. "All we have to do is get rid of the Cats that show up at the meeting." Portia thought the voice must be the leader of the Serpents. Any orphan who lived long enough to get old usually rose to leadership positions. "The Hares won't touch us. They're in on this," the voice responded to an unheard protest. Her stomach clenched as she realized she was right: the meeting was a trap. She grimaced as she turned to Mark. His pale face told her that he had heard the same thing.

"What Cats do they think will show up?" A different voice asked.

"Deyelna—the leader—and probably some of her enforcers. And the ones we're supposed to get rid of," the leader responded. "Don't hurt Deyelna... she's the one funding this." Mark inhaled sharply. Portia turned and motioned for him to be quiet.

A soft whistle came from someone below. A third voice spoke. "She's paying to betray her own gang? That's the most cold-blooded thing I've ever heard of." There were mutters of agreement.

"There is someone else... an anti-magicker. Our plant in the Hares said he's been meeting with Deyelna. He's been flashing gold around and promising things for the skins of certain magickers," the leader said.

Silence greeted this pronouncement. Portia sucked in her breath. The anti-magickers were a dangerous lot. They had burned a young girl alive in the city last fall—a girl they claimed was possessed by evil spirits. The city guard had driven them out, but apparently they were not all gone. What could Deyelna be doing with one of them? Deyelna was not anti-magic, at least not when it came to her own abilities.

The volume of the voices went down, making it difficult to pick out any words. Portia leaned in, trying to hear anything, considering whether they should get closer.

A rasping noise came from behind her. She spun in irritation to quiet Mark again when she saw one of his feet had slipped—he was hanging precariously by one knee and a hand and sliding quickly off. She clutched the rafter tightly with her legs and leaned forward, grabbing him with both arms. Mark's weight almost pulled her off the beam, but she had a tight enough grip with her legs as to not tumble over. She stopped Mark's motion. They clung to the beam, waiting a second before pulling Mark back up again. As they hung there, Portia felt something slip from one of her pockets. A caltrop fell to the boxes below, skittering and sliding until it went off the top of the boxes into the open space where the meeting was being held. Portia swore under her breath.

Exclamations and yells came from the meeting spot.

Two young men ran out into the path that led to the open spot through the boxes and looked up, spotting Mark and Portia. "Get them!" the leader yelled.

Portia pulled Mark all the way up.

They ran towards the far end of the warehouse, passing the mass of boxes below. Portia pulled out her rope and quickly tied it around the rafter, dropping it down. She shimmied down the rope. Mark followed. Luckily, the boxes acted as a barrier and a maze to the Serpents who were trying to reach them. They could hear their voices, but none were visible yet.

Mark and Portia ran to the exterior warehouse door that was near them. Right before the door, Portia slowed to a walk, and motioned for Mark to do the same. She opened the door and walked out casually, nodding at the two Serpents stationed outside. They nodded back. Mark did the same.

Portia's heart was beating so loudly she was sure the Serpents could have heard it. She walked as quickly as she could while still acting casually. Instead of saying anything about Mark and Portia, the Serpent guards continued a discussion of the day's race results. Apparently, Peter was not the only one who had lost money that day.

A yell and a pounding on the exterior door stopped the guards' chatter. Serpents burst from within the warehouse. They spied Mark and Portia halfway down the block, tearing after them.

Mark and Portia ran.

They cleared a corner, escaping the direct vision of the Serpents chasing them. "Get on the roof and go back to the den," Portia said to Mark. "I'll lead them away." Mark protested, but Portia knew there was no other way. He was not as fast as she was. Besides, there was no point in both of them getting caught. She shoved him at a ladder as they passed it. "Go!"

Mark scrambled up the ladder up onto the roof while Portia slowed her running slightly. Mark disappeared over the edge of the roof just as the Serpents came around the corner. Portia breathed a sigh of relief while she jogged in place, waiting for the Serpents to see her. When they yelled and pointed her way, she took off at top speed towards the Lynx territory. She wanted the Serpents to think it was anyone but Black Cats spying on them. Even better, the Lynxes were bitter enemies of the Serpents. She hoped that would be enough to slow down their pursuit.

She ran until she spied a dark alley coming up on her left. She quickly checked that the alley had an exit and turned into it. She grabbed her bag of caltrops, dumped them into her hand, and then threw them across the opening of the alley before running to the far end. Cries of pain echoed behind her as the pursuing Serpents found her present for them. She kept running. Footsteps came from behind her, but not as many as before.

The warehouses gave way to the brick buildings of the smiths. She ran one block in, then slowed, doing her best to walk casually. She mentally plotted a route back to the Black Cat den. There were more people out than in the warehouse district. Portia wished she had the magic of invisibility. Looking down, her hand seemed to shimmer into nothing. She blinked, and when she looked again, the effect was gone. She thought it must be wishful thinking. Shaking her head with a grimace, she put all her concentration back on the problem of getting home.

"Hey, Orphan," a voice greeted her. Portia looked up to notice another orphan. This one had the orange Lynx tag on the right sleeve of his jacket. She quickly tucked in the collar of her jacket that had the Black Cat black patch, trying to pass the motion off as scratching her neck. He smiled at her. She couldn't tell if he had noticed what she had done, but he was definitely friendlier than the gang chasing her.

She walked over to him, considered what she might say, while also keeping an eye out for her pursuers. Before she had her thoughts together, the Lynx was already speaking. "What are you doing here? Are you lost?" he asked.

"I'm trying to get away from some Serpents—"

Portia jumped as the Serpents chasing her turned the corner into the Smithing district. The Lynx orphan turned to see what she was looking at. He gave the intruders a dark look. He grabbed Portia and pushed her towards the open door of the smithy.

"Grab the horn on the doorframe and bring it here," he yelled. Portia did as she was told, feeling a tingle from the smooth bone horn as she pulled it off the hook where it was hanging, then ran to bring it to the Lynx. She felt magic emanating from it.

The Lynx orphan took the horn from her. He turned to face the oncoming Serpents, took a deep inhale, then blew into the horn. Curls of orange, yellow, and white-hot fire exploded out of the horn and shot down the street towards the Serpents. One Serpent yelped in pain as the fire engulfed his feet, but most of them ran around the sides towards Portia and the Lynx. Portia despaired that she would never lose them all.

But the horn also had the effect of calling other nearby Lynx gang members.

Lynx orphans came running from all directions around them. The pursuing Serpents and the gathering Lynx collided in a mass in front of the smithy. Portia watched wide-eyed as they started fist fighting, her presence apparently forgotten.

Portia backed up slowly. She didn't want to get involved in the fight; she didn't know what magic the Serpents, or the Lynx, had. It might look like a simple scuffle, but there could be more involved that she couldn't see. She felt her back touch the smithy wall.

She slid to the right, keeping an eye on the brawling orphans, until she found the corner of the building. Then she passed around the corner and ran to the end of the next block and took a sharp left. She was trying to get as much distance as possible between her and the fighting gang members. She ran until her side hurt and then stopped, stooped over panting, and watched for pursuers.

No one came after her.

When she stood up, a motion caught her eye on the rooftop of the building across from her. She thought she saw a face. It had looked like Peter. She frowned. What was he doing here? Was he spying on her? Or was there some other reason for him to be in the Smithing district? Her heart constricted when she thought of the conspiracy against the Black Cats. Peter was Deyelna's right-hand man. Did he know about it? Was he a part of it?

Portia decided to find out the quickest way possible. She saw a fire escape on the building Peter was standing on top of halfway down the block. She jogged to it then climbed rapidly to the roof. She didn't want Peter getting away.

When she got to the roof, Peter was waiting with his arms crossed. He was not trying to hide his presence at all.

"Are you following me?" she asked.

Peter looked at her calmly. He raised his chin at her, acknowledging her question. "Yes."

Portia waited for more. Peter walked towards her. "I was following you. I saw you send Mark away. Deyelna's orders were clear—you are both to go to the warehouse district." Portia's heart sank. He *was* here spying for Deyelna.

"We did both go. We barely got away. I sent Mark away so that if someone got caught, it would just be me." Portia said.

"You had a task to accomplish there," Peter said accusingly.

"We accomplished it," Portia said. She wasn't sure how much she should tell Peter. Did he know everything?

Peter eyed her skeptically. "You know I have to report that claim back to Deyelna, right?"

Portia lifted her chin defiantly. Her heart was pounding in fear, but she didn't want Peter to know that.

Peter frowned. He hesitated, and then looked left and right. Not seeing anyone, he stepped in closer to Portia. "She's planning on getting rid of both you and Mark. I never understood why."

Portia felt ill. It was just as she had suspected. Her resolve weakened; she lowered her head to stare at his feet. "I know why," she said in a low voice. "It's because her magic doesn't work on me." She looked to see if Peter knew what she was talking about. He nodded. "She can't charm me into doing what she wants—and it infuriates her."

Peter sighed, exasperated. Before he could say anything, Portia pushed on. "It's not just that. Deyelna is trying to get rid of some Black Cats. I don't think it's just me and Mark—"

Peter held up a hand, stopping her from going further. "I know of her magic too. You didn't really think I do what I do because she charmed me, did you? Nevermind, don't answer that." Peter paced around her. "I know about her plan. Don't speak of it to me again."

Portia frowned. What was Peter's endgame? Was he so sure that Deyelna wouldn't betray him too? "Why are you still working with her then?" Portia asked.

"That isn't your business," Peter said, and then he disappeared in a blink of light. Portia realized she had been talking to his duplicate, and he had not really been there at all. It took an extraordinary amount of energy to project himself so far from the den. She wondered why he had done so. Perhaps he wasn't so sure of his safety from the Serpents and the Lynx after all. She shook her head. She couldn't worry about that now. She had to get back to protect Mark.

4

ortia made it back to the Black Cat den without running into any other orphans. When she got back, no one had been guarding the door. That was not a good sign. She quickly dashed through the halls to the room she and Mark shared. Mark lay on the bed bouncing a ball against the wall, waiting for her.

"Are you okay?" Mark asked. He put the ball away. He only bounced it when he was anxious. Portia had previously asked him not to do that since it irritated the other Black Cats, but it was a compulsion he couldn't always control.

"I am. But we need to leave here quickly," Portia said. She had not forgotten Deyelna's plans for them. Glancing at Mark, she saw the sour look on his face and knew he hadn't forgotten it either. It must have taken a lot of willpower to sit here waiting for her while his gang leader was plotting his demise.

"Did you have any problems getting back?" Portia asked

as she walked to her chest, throwing it open. She grabbed her bag of caltrops—there were only a few dozen left. She shoved the entire lot into her shoulder bag. There was a good chance they would not be in this room again, and weapons were hard to come by. "Come on, we need to pack." Portia said as she turned to Mark.

Mark shook his head. "Guess who helped me get back to the den?" Mark said, waiting for Portia's response. When she said nothing, he volunteered. "Peter."

Portia frowned. What game was Peter playing? He was spying for Deyelna, yet also telling Portia things she was pretty sure she was not supposed to know. Portia shook her head to clear her thoughts. She'd have to figure that out later. She motioned to Mark to pack up. She stopped when she saw Peter and two enforcers standing in the doorway watching them.

Mark turned to see what Portia was looking at. Peter crossed his arms, looking down his nose at them. "Deyelna wants to see you two," he said. The enforcers behind him jostled for a view, waiting to see if Mark and Portia resisted. Apparently, there was not enough excitement around there for them lately. "We're going to the throne room. Now."

Portia considered whether she and Mark could make a break for it. She looked at the size of the enforcers and decided not—at least not with them blocking the door.

"We can do this by force if need be," Peter said, as he glanced at the two enforcers behind him, "or not. The choice is up to you."

Portia swallowed. Peter and the enforcers were more than

enough to take on her and Mark—even if Peter didn't use his duplicating magic. She needed to buy some time to come up with a plan. She willed her breathing to steady, then sighed for effect. "Fine," she said, trying to sound nonchalant. She made eye contact with Mark as they followed Peter out the door. Mark nodded subtly back at her.

The halls of the house were strangely empty. Peter led them to the rear of the house where Deyelna's throne room and den was located. The two enforcers with him trailed behind them, blocking their exit. Portia was sure they would welcome an escape attempt. She wondered what Deyelna had told them about her.

When they reached Deyelna's room, Peter opened the door, and Portia saw all the members of the Black Cat gang waiting inside. Deyelna was lounging on her throne. Everyone turned to face her and Mark as they entered the room. The loud talking died off until the room was silent. Deyelna motioned Portia and Mark to step forward. Peter pushed them forward towards Deyelna when they did not move fast enough.

Deyelna allowed the silence to hang, heightening the anticipation. Portia looked around the crowd. She spied Merwin, whom she knew considered himself neutral. Even he avoided her eye contact, letting his dreads block his eyes from her. Portia checked for sympathetic faces and found none—those in the crowd who did not avoid eye contact stared at her and Mark with naked anticipation. This was a trial, but Mark and Portia did not have a single defender.

"So, you've returned," Deyelna said, "your mission accomplished. At least that's what you reported to Peter." The last part of her statement dripped with sarcasm. When Portia and Mark didn't respond, Deyelna then looked to Peter. "Isn't that right, Peter?" Peter nodded. Deyelna turned to face Portia once again. "And what mission might that be, Portia?" Deyelna asked as she slowly rose from her throne, as she ran her thumb over her fingers in the direction of the watching Black Cats, who murmured in response. Portia knew Deyelna was using her charm spell on the gang. It would not matter what they said in response to Deyelna: no one there would believe her. They were all under Deyelna's control.

"Look at these two," Deyelna continued. "They are so blatant. So brazen. They walk right in the door of *our* home, as if they were not out busy betraying us all." The crowd muttered.

"That's not true!" Mark said. Portia grabbed his arm to stop him, but he shook her off. "We heard it, you're the one betraying us! We heard the Serpents discussing—"

"Liar!" Deyelna said, pointing at Mark. Deyelna turned to the crowd. "What do we do with liars? And traitors?" The crowd roared in response.

"I'm not a liar!" Mark said. The crowd jeered at him.

Portia saw Deyelna rubbing the fingers on both hands in the direction of the crowd. Everywhere Deyelna pointed, the volume of the crowd increased. She was feeding their anger and paranoia. She had complete control of them.

Mark stepped towards Deyelna, trying to get her attention. Portia grabbed Mark and pulled him close before Deyelna noticed. She whispered loudly in his ear. "Stop!

They won't listen. Use your magic on my signal. Full strength. *Full!*" Portia pulled back when Deyelna turned to face them again.

Deyelna walked closer, circling Portia and Mark, while her gang jeered on. Portia tried one last time to make eye contact with anyone in the crowd, but there was not a single friendly face. Deyelna stopped in front of her, blocking her view. She stepped in so close to Portia that Portia could feel the heat off Deyelna's body and see the redness in her eyes.

"Are you taking one last look at the people you were betraying?" Deyelna asked. "Does it make you feel like a strong person? Well you're not; you're weak. And I don't tolerate weakness in my gang. Or cowards." Deyelna turned once again to the crowd. "Do I?" she asked them. They yelled *no* in unison. Portia felt ill as she heard cries of "get them" and "kill them" from the crowd. She had thought some of these orphans were her friends. Even though she knew it was Deyelna's magic, it still felt like a betrayal.

While Deyelna's back was to her, Portia looked to Mark and gave him the nod to use his magic. He nodded back. Portia screwed her eyes shut as tightly as she could just as the room erupted into a blinding light. Portia heard howls of pain from the Black Cat members in the room as the light hit them, searing their retinas. She grabbed Mark and made a dash for the exit. She ran into someone on the way, shoving them down. She realized it was Peter when she heard his grunt as he landed on the floor. Good. That should at least slow him down a bit.

Portia and Mark ran from the room. "Flash your light

whenever someone gets too close," Portia yelled, pulling Mark towards the front door.

"I'll try," Mark said. Portia knew it exhausted Mark to use magic. They had limited time to get away. Mark tried to turn them towards their room. "We should get our stuff," he said.

"No. It's too dangerous. We need to get out of here, quickly." Portia said. Mark turned to face behind them and used his light once again to stop the few Black Cats who had recovered and were coming after them. Portia saw the light flash down the front hall, and it hurt even when she wasn't directly looking at it. She dragged Mark backwards towards the front door as he kept flashing their pursuers. She squinted to avoid as much of the light herself as possible. She felt Mark get slower as they went, his energy draining. They had to get away—and quickly.

They burst out of the front door and ran down the street towards the butcher shop. Portia pulled Mark behind the racks in front that normally held barrels of preserved meat during the day as a few Black Cats ran past, not seeing them hiding there. Portia guessed they were still seeing stars from Mark's magic, and their vision wasn't as good as it normally was. As soon as the pursuers ran past, Portia and Mark came out again and continued down the street. Portia decided the safest thing to do was to get out of the city. Deyelna had the Serpents in on her plan. Who knew who else was involved? They had to escape.

"We have to get out of a city gate," Portia yelled to Mark as they ran. He nodded back, breathing raggedly. He was having a hard time keeping up after using so much of his magic. "Stick together," Portia said.

She knew Mark had never been out of the city, and she didn't want him to run into worse trouble out there without her. She'd heard stories of the wandering thieves who roamed outside the city walls. Their ruthlessness was often the subject of market gossip. She hoped the tales were exaggerations but feared they were not. Mark didn't bother responding to her last instructions—he was struggling to breathe as they ran.

Portia and Mark turned the corner and nearly ran into a roving band of Serpent orphans. Portia recognized the tall Serpent leader from the warehouse. Worse yet, he recognized her. He yelled and pointed. The Serpents ran towards Mark and Portia.

Mark and Portia veered to the right to escape the chasing gang. Portia led. She turned and saw hands reaching out for Mark, who was trailing behind her. He was too tired to use his magic ability to blind their pursuers. She stopped running to allow Mark to pass, then kicked the first pursuer in the chest, pushing him into the rest of the Serpents and knocking them all over. She ran after Mark, swiftly catching up to him. They ran on, trying to reach the west gate, which was the closest city gate to the Black Cat den. Portia considered running through the Lynx Smithing district but decided the safest way was to try to skirt along the boundaries of the Smithing and Warehouse districts. She hoped all the Serpents were in the Black Cat territory looking for her and Mark.

Unfortunately, not all the Black Cats were in the Black

Cat territory. She recognized two orphans from their den ahead of her. She tugged on Mark's sleeve to get his attention, but he was too tired to look up. The Black Cats spied them before Portia could pull Mark into a hiding spot. They rushed at Mark and Portia. In a panic, Portia pushed Mark down a narrow alley she knew only he could pass through, while running in the opposite direction. The two Black Cats looked between Portia and Mark and then both followed Mark into the alley. Portia knew the Black Cats were too large to pass through the narrow opening at the end of the alleyway—they were older, nearly enforcer age. She just hoped Mark had enough energy to get there before they caught him. She knew he would run towards a city gate. She'd have to meet him there.

Portia was desperate to not run into any more pursuers. She was getting tired and feared she'd make mistakes. The pain in her side was so great she had to stop running. She would not be able to run the entire way to the city gate.

She decided to go south, around the far side of the Serpent Warehouse district, to reach the west gate. It would take longer. Perhaps she could get there by walking instead of running and hiding the entire way. The sun should be up by the time she got there, and she hoped she could blend into the crowds once there.

Portia ran along the rooftops of the Warehouse district as she passed through it on her way to the far side. Luckily, she didn't run into a single Serpent.

Reaching the west gate, she noticed with a curse that it was closed and locked. The guards were there, making sure no one defied the will of the city planners by opening this gate before sunrise. She looked to the sky in the east—it was pink. Sunrise would happen soon. At least she knew Mark had not already passed through this way. She decided to ask the guards if they'd seen him anyhow. There were three other gates he could have gone to, and she would be hard-pressed to reach them all quickly. She didn't want the Serpents or Black Cats—or the bandits outside the city—to get to Mark while she was searching for him.

Portia did not recognize the guards. They were not ones she had befriended or accidentally dropped coins for in the past. She checked her appearance quickly. She hid the gang symbol by tucking her collar deep inside her shirt.

Looking around the street, Portia searched for a prop she could use. She needed a reason to be there, otherwise they would suspect she was an orphan. The orphans were tolerated by the city elite, for now, mostly because it was too difficult to decide what to do with them all. But they were not favored. If the orphans had not decided to stick together in gangs, they would not survive long in the city of Valencia. It would be much better to show up with a basket as a farmer's daughter who had come to the market to sell produce than as an orphan. But Portia only saw a broken bucket with a hole in the bottom discarded in the street. It would have to do. She grabbed it and hoped it was dark enough that the guard wouldn't notice its uselessness. She would have to be polite and meek as she imagined a farmer's daughter would be, instead of giving off the surly toughness most gang members tried to project for their own survival.

Approaching the nearest guard, she noticed he was exhausted and yawning, with a heavy chin growth. These must still be the night guards. This was a stroke in her favor—they had not changed shifts yet.

"Pardon me, sir," she said to the guard, trying to get his attention. "Have you seen my brother? He's about fifteen hands high."

The guard gave her a particular look. "Is your brother a horse?" he asked with a smirk.

Portia realized she had said things incorrectly. Apparently only orphans described their own heights that way. "No, of course not... Sir. Well, he sort of does eat like one." Her face turned red.

The guard noticed her embarrassment and softened a little. He chuckled. "Ay, I have a boy. You're not wrong—they do eat like horses. What does he look like, besides being fifteen hands high?"

"He's blond, thin. Eleven years old..."

"No, haven't seen anyone like that this night. It's not safe for kids at night here. You shouldn't be out early yourself. Where are your parents?" The guard looked at her more closely, waking up a bit, alertness coming into his eyes.

"Oh, they're coming. They should be coming along soon," Portia said, waving in the general direction of the city behind her while backing up. "Thank you so much for your help." She turned and stepped away quickly before the guard could ask any more questions.

So, Mark had not been to the west gate. That was not a good sign since it was the closest one. She hoped he'd only been deflected by pursuers and decided to try another gate. Or maybe he had stopped somewhere safe for rest. They had not slept all night, and she knew he was exhausted from using his magic for their escape. She refused to think about what would have happened to him if the Black Cats or Serpents had caught him.

The next closest gate he might have gone to was the north gate. Her stomach hurt at the thought of going there. The north gate was much closer to Serpent territory. The last thing she wanted to do was to go back that way, but she couldn't leave Mark behind. She squared her shoulders and turned towards the warehouse district and her goal of the gate behind it.

She left the west gate area just as the sun was rising. She could hear the new guards arriving and changing over as she walked away. The gate creaked as they cranked it open. She wanted more than anything to be outside the gate and away from the city, but she was torn—Mark was still inside somewhere.

It was growing late enough in the morning that the merchants were up and about, loading their wagons and starting the day's business. It was easier for her to be inconspicuous now, but it would also be easier for the Serpents to hide from her as she passed through their territory. She would just have to be more vigilant. She found a wagon that was going north and tagged along behind it.

The wagon passed about halfway through the Warehouse district before it turned off towards the east, leaving her vulnerable. Portia watched it drive away, uncertain. She could either follow it east, which would take her away from where she wanted to go, or she could strike off alone through the streets. Portia finally decided it was more important to get to Mark quickly. Cautiously she walked north between warehouses looking for Serpents as well as another ladder to the rooftops where she could run faster, away from so many spying eyes.

She spied a metal ladder at the end of the block she was on and walked towards it. Before she could reach it, she heard a yell from behind and turned to see two Serpent orphans running towards her. She sprinted down the street to the ladder, dodging between merchants on the street. The adults swore as she bounced off them. One particularly irate man grabbed her by her upper arm, and she had to kick him in the shin to get him to release his grip. He howled in rage as she slipped away.

Unfortunately, it had given the Serpents time to catch up to her before she reached the ladder. One of them had a long wooden club that was embedded with metal bits. He swung the club at her shoulder. It made impact. Pain seared down Portia's arm and along her neck. She bit back a scream, concentrating on running from the Serpents. The Serpent with the club ran after her, winding up for another blow. His companion wisely stayed clear of the swinging weapon.

Portia thought about Mark's blinding flashes. She wished with all her heart that Mark was there to blind these two. She didn't think she was fast enough to get away. And there didn't appear to be any Lynx orphans around to save her this time.

Suddenly, behind her, a flash erupted. The Serpents

yelled, as did merchants and citizens who were out in the street. They had also been caught in the light blast. Men and women on the street were bent over, hands on their eyes. Luckily, Portia had been facing away from it and could still see.

She squinted in case another blast was coming and ran to the ladder. She gripped it in her sweating hands then raced up it as fast as she could to the rooftop. Once she was safely on top of the building, she ran across the roof to the far edge of the building. There was a ten-foot gap between the buildings. Portia looked at the gap. It was frighteningly large. But she had no choice unless she wanted to get caught and forced back to face Deyelna. Portia ran back for a running start and then tore across the roof towards the gap. She jumped with all her strength.

She landed with a thump on her belly on the edge of the roof. Scrabbling with her hands, she got a hold of the brick facade, then pulled herself up on to the roof. Her stomach hurt terribly where she had hit the bricks. She breathed in tentatively, relieved when she didn't feel any broken ribs.

Checking the roof she had just come from, she didn't see anyone following her. They might not have even seen her climb up to it if they were still blinded by the intense light. She breathed a small sigh of relief.

Where had the blast come from? Mark was the only one she knew of who could do that. Was he around? She scanned all the rooftops but didn't see anybody. Carefully peering over the edge of the building, she couldn't see Mark anywhere in the crowd. Surely if he was there and had helped her he would have made himself known to her.

Could she have had anything to do with the light flash? She had been thinking about Mark's magic when it happened. A feeling tickled along her spine. She had done several types of magic before, always under duress it seemed, and she had been puzzled how she could do more than one. That was not something she had heard about from any of the other orphans: people, if they could do magic at all, could only do one kind. She had not mentioned her abilities to anyone in the Black Cats for fear Deyelna would find out about it. She did not need Deyelna to have one more reason to hate her—being immune to the Black Cats leader's magic was bad enough.

Portia looked one more time for Mark. He was not anywhere to be seen. Pulling herself back from the edge of the building, she picked her way along the rooftops towards the north gate. The sun was quickly ascending the sky, and the gate would be packed with merchants coming in and going out, mixing with the farmers bringing their wares to market. The north gate was the busiest gate in the entire city. It would be difficult at best to find Mark there.

When she got to the north gate, it was worse than she feared. The gate itself was packed with people coming and going—the courtyard in front of the gate was full of wagons, carts, horses, people, baskets, and all manner of goods for that day's market. Some men were so tall that they obscured her view and she had a difficult time even seeing across the courtyard. She looked for a rooftop to get a better view, but there were no nearby buildings. Part of the city's defense was to keep structures away from the walls surrounding the city. This prevented aggressors from throwing fire over the walls and reaching a building. These were lessons city planners had learned over millennia of fighting—at least that is what Portia had heard from the elder orphans. She didn't understand who they had been fighting since there had been peace for as long as she could remember.

She sighed, giving up on the idea of a view from above. She decided to approach the guards again at this gate. Even though they were probably new guards for the day—all the guards for the night usually retired with the sunrise—they still might have seen Mark. Perhaps she would get lucky and find a guard that she knew. She needed an ally in this quest.

Pushing through the crowd, she got halfway across the courtyard when she tripped over a goose that had gotten loose from its pen. Cursing, she stumbled and looked behind her to see who the animal belonged to. As she turned, she glimpsed two Peters coming towards her. Her heart raced. He and his duplicate would have been able to sneak up on her if she hadn't stumbled and seen them just by chance. She looked around for a quick escape or a place to hide, but Peter was too close. He would see wherever she tried to hide.

She bolted east since it was the clearest direction. She got as far as she could until she turned a corner and ran into a wagon full of hay that was surrounded by people. She scanned for a way around the unexpected obstacle. Peter had gained on her—both of him. They would be upon her within a minute. She stared back at Peter in horror and then scrunched up her eyes and thought of Mark. She imagined his light moats at their most brilliant: she imagined the brightness of the sun.

The flash of light was so intense it hurt her even with her eyes squeezed shut. She heard the crash of a wagon as its horses abruptly stopped and refused to move, whinnying in pain. Opening her eyes, she saw people bent over double, hands pressed to their eyes, even Peter—both of him. She wondered if the double Peter really had hurt eyes or if it was just a projection from whichever one was the real Peter. Neither one of them was looking at her. This was her chance.

She didn't want Peter to keep running after her. If she could really do other magic, like Mark's magic of light moats and flashes, perhaps she could do Peter's magic too. If she could have a double of her own, she could send it running off in the wrong direction and have Peter chase it.

She quickly ducked behind a wagon, putting it between her and the Peters. Closing her eyes, she imagined a second Portia. She imagined her double on the other side of the wagon, closer to the gate. She felt a weakness in her hands and feet; her knees buckled a bit. She grabbed a hold of the wagon to steady herself. She opened her eyes and peered around the wagon towards the Peters. She gasped. Just past the Peters, looking back at her, she saw a clone of herself. She thought she was looking at a mirror. She raised her right arm, testing, but the clone did not raise its right arm in response. She willed the clone to back up two steps—and it did. Her heart soared in elation. She could do it! The thrill of victory almost made up for the drain of the energy she had to use to maintain the clone.

The Peters were looking around, their eyesight having recovered. Portia ducked down behind the wagon again. She willed her clone to throw a stone at one of the Peters to draw their attention. It must have worked because she heard a yelp from their direction. Peeking out from the wagon again, she saw the Peters turn in the direction of her clone. She willed it to run out the gate, weaving in and out between pedestrians and road traffic. She didn't know if it felt solid to the touch, so tried to guide it away from coming too close to other people. She wished she had paid more attention to Peter's magic. She couldn't remember if she had ever touched Peter's clone, or if she seen anyone else do so. He did not use that trick all that often—at least not in the Black Cat den.

The duplicate got farther into the gate area, finally disappearing outside and out of Portia's view. She gave it two more seconds, watching the Peters continue to run after it, before releasing the spell. She was so exhausted from maintaining it, she could barely breathe. She wondered if she could die from running a spell too long. Could it drain all her life force?

When she let go of the spell, both of the Peters stopped running. They hesitated for just a second, then continued running in the direction her duplicate had been heading before disappearing. Portia thought she had seen one of the Peters' neck stiffen when he had stopped, as if he was going to look around and forced himself to not do so. Was someone watching him? She looked around in a panic for any other spying orphans.

5

Portia didn't see any watching orphans in the north gate area. That didn't mean they weren't there. She had to get out and away from the north gate as quickly as possible. She made her way east, looking out for Mark as she went. She went past a butcher's stall, swiping a piece of salt pork from a barrel while the butcher was distracted with a mother and her two screaming kids. Tears were running down the children's faces. Portia felt bad when she realized they were probably crying from the bright flash in the courtyard by the gate—the light flash that she had caused.

She knew that disruptive magic was frowned on by the city guards and captain. They would surely lock her up and bring her in front of a judge if they knew she was the one who had caused the disturbance. Things did not go well for orphans who made it in front of judges. She knew of Black Cats who had been brought in front of one and never came back. No one knew for certain what happened to them. Even the gate guards didn't seem to know.

She chewed on the salt pork as she walked towards the harbor gate. She was grateful for the food. Between staying up all night and using so much magic, she was exhausted. Her head felt weak, and her feet tingled as she walked.

Passing down the street, she spied a hat in the back of a wagon parked there. She checked and seeing that the wagon's driver was distracted looking at the foot of one of his horses, she swiped the hat as she passed by, tucking it into her jacket. Once she turned the next corner, she put the hat on her head, pulling it down low to hide her eyes. The hat smelled of fresh hay and farm waste. She wrinkled her nose but did not remove it. She tucked her hair inside to further change her appearance. She was too tired to run. Hopefully, no one would recognize her with this small disguise. She wished she had a different jacket than her old dingy one. The Black Cats would easily recognize it even if it was turned inside out.

She quickly finished the piece of meat she had stolen and regretted not getting more when she could. Her stomach growled, but there were no stands to steal from between the city markets. The streets were still relatively quiet as most of the city was not up yet.

Reaching the harbor market, she scanned for Mark. There were fewer people than yesterday even though the royal ship was still in the harbor. Perhaps the populace was bored with its presence when nothing exciting had happened yesterday. They no longer hoped for a glimpse of a royal.

She also looked for Brown Hares: the harbor market was

their territory. Worse yet, they were now somehow in league with Deyelna. Portia wished she still had the letter she had stolen from the Hare, but Deyelna now had it. It might have been useful. Or perhaps it was for the best to no longer have it in her possession. Portia shivered involuntarily at what might happen if she was caught with it by a Hare—or worse yet, a Serpent. Surely, the boy she had stolen it from knew it was missing by now.

Portia wandered over to the pastry stall, looking for Mark and any other orphans while considering if it was worth the risk of stealing a pastry. The last thing she should be doing right now is taking another chance, but she was extremely hungry. Her mind was demanding food. But before she could get closer to the stall, she spied Merwin's head of black dreadlocks. He was turning and scanning the crowd. Portia could have sworn that he saw her, but he kept turning, his eyes passing over her and continuing to look. He walked off in the direction of the water. If Merwin was here, then there was a chance there were other Black Cats as well.

Portia turned, scanning the crowd, and saw four Black Cat orphans directly behind her and approaching her fast. They must have been following her. The one in front made eye contact with Portia as he ran forward to grab her. Portia put up one hand to deflect him, squeezed her eyes shut, and summoned a light flash. But she was weak. The flash was not bright enough to blind all of them, but the lead Cat stumbled and rubbed his eyes.

Portia pulled out some caltrops from her bag and threw them on the ground in front of the remaining three Black

Cats. She turned and fled towards the ships in the harbor. Two of the Black Cats could not stop themselves in time and they stepped on the sharp metal caltrops she had thrown on the ground. They bounced on one foot in pain, and one of them fell to the ground, blood streaming from his shoe.

Portia heard the last Black Cat running after her. She hurried her pace as much as she could, a sharp pain in her side pulling with each step.

She veered towards the docks, not thinking. She ran down the wooden structure, feeling it bounce with her weight. The vast ocean in front of her terrified her, but her pursuer was now between her and solid land. She ran further down the dock hoping to find an escape on a ship somehow. Ahead, she spied a gangplank coming down from a large galleon. Running up the plank, she nearly collided with a sailor at the top. He yelled in surprise and outrage and tried to grab her. She evaded his hands. Running across the ship, she also avoided the other sailors who were yelling at her intrusion and scrambling after her.

There was an adjacent ship on the other side, but it was too far to jump over the gap in between them. She spied a rope towards the rear of the ship and ran towards it. The Black Cat pursuing her reached the top of the gangplank just as she reached the rope. He saw her and sprinted in her direction.

Grabbing the rope, Portia took a running start towards the other ship. The Black Cat adjusted his pursuit to intercept her path. He would have reached her too—before she was able to swing over to the other ship—but a sailor grabbed a hold of the orphan's jacket and slowed him down just enough for her run by. She held on tightly to the rope while she ran off the deck towards the other ship. She swung out over the water. Reaching the height of the rope's arc, she closed her eyes and let go, hoping she had enough momentum to land on the next ship's deck. After what seemed an eternity, she landed with a thud, rolling across the deck. She had made it. The Black Cat behind her did not. He had tried to jump the gap and was not able to get to the other side. He fell into the ocean with a splash.

Portia ran past the surprised faces of the sailors on the second ship. She found their gangplank. Thankfully, it was extended to the dock below. She ran down it and turned on the dock towards the shore before any of the sailors had reacted to grab her.

Portia ran through the harbor market, all thoughts of grabbing more food gone. She headed towards the last city gate—surely the Black Cats weren't guarding them all.

The city was waking up. The streets were more crowded. Portia struggled to make good time as she had to walk around the people in the streets while looking out for wagons and pickpockets. The surest safety was to have a good distance between herself and others. She knew from personal experience how innocent a thief could look.

She was halfway to the next gate when she saw another Black Cat on the street behind her. She forced herself to move faster, trying to keep out of sight as much as possible, keeping wagons and groups of people between herself and the Black Cat as much as possible. She hoped she had not been recognized. The Black Cat behind her was a younger female orphan, who had just joined the gang last year; she was not as bold as others. She was also tiny at ten years old. Even if she had spotted Portia, more than likely she was waiting for reinforcements. The best thing would be to lose her before those reinforcements came.

Portia considered laying down the rest of her caltrops but decided against it. She had just a few left. It was better to save them for emergencies. Besides, there were too many regular citizens out who might step on them while the Black Cat behind her could easily avoid them once alerted to their presence.

When she reached the gate, she realized she had been herded there. There were at least five Black Cats spaced around the courtyard in front of the gate. She picked them out of the crowd quickly, even with the crush of vendors and farmers and guards. Three years of working the street as a thief had sharpened her eyes for friend and foe alike.

Another figure caught her eye—a tall man all in black. The crowd scattered out of his way. Portia's heart thumped. He looked like the man that had chased her and Mark from the harbor market. Could he be the anti-magicker they'd overheard discussed in the warehouse meeting? The Black Cat members ignored the man, neither avoiding him nor joining him. Portia chilled at the strange behavior. Goosebumps rose on her arms. He passed out of the courtyard. She breathed a sigh of relief. He scared her more than the gang members.

The Black Cats had spied her. They moved towards her, constricting their circle. Portia saw a large wagon train exiting the gate, the guards holding the swinging metal doors open for them. She ran for the gap between the guard and the front wagon—flashing light moats at the two nearest Black Cats who tried to grab her. She thought that was the last of her energy for magic, at least for now. She had to get out. She had to rest.

She turned sideways as she slipped between the guard and the wagon. The guard looked surprised and then infuriated. He had no reason to grab her except that she was running, but that was enough to trigger his instincts. He ran ten steps after her before looking back at his now-abandoned post at the gate. Cursing, he went back to his duty, giving up the pursuit.

Portia ran down the hill away from the city and over the next crest towards the forest that lay just over it away from the city. The wagons on the road behind her creaked and rumbled, then the noise faded into nothing as she ran from them. There was no one around her on the gravel road. As she passed over the crest, she felt the silence of the country and the nearby forest. It was so different from the city. The lack of sound was smothering. There were no calls of vendors, no children screaming, no mothers calling, no sounds of wagons on the city's brick streets.

She slowed, her heart pounding, gasping for breath. She looked around for a place to hide. There was only the forest before her, dark and foreboding. Otherwise, the country was open, not a building or even a boulder to hide behind.

She grasped her hands into fists then walked resolutely

towards the forest. She wouldn't go in far, but she did have to get out of sight from the road.

Entering the forest, the cool shade felt good. She realized she was soaked in sweat. Taking off her hat, she used it to fan herself. She walked behind a large tree. Leaning against it, she slid down to sit at its base.

After a few moments, when the pounding of her heart receded, sounds began to fill her ears. Birds were singing. The faint call of crickets came from the nearby countryside. A small furry animal scampered by. This made her feel a bit better about the forest. She hoped if the small creatures were out then nothing more dangerous was around.

She rested there until the growling of her stomach forced her to think about what to do next. She couldn't just stay there. Besides the issue of eating, there was her safety. It felt okay in the forest in the morning, but what would it be like at night? Who knew what lurked in the dark woods. Also, she had to find Mark. Much as she was loath to move, staying was not an option. At least not right now.

Looking back at the hill that hid the city, she got up and dusted herself off. The Black Cats had not followed her outside the gate, not that she could see. Perhaps they were under orders not to. She knew that if she had not been desperate, she would not have exited the city either. Most of the orphans in the Black Cats had never stepped one foot outside of Valencia—their parents had disappeared, or died, leaving the children to survive, or not, as they could. Other cities had enough of their own orphans, she had heard. The guards would not let more in the gate if they could help it.

She walked back towards Valencia. There were vendors that had set themselves up outside the city walls. Perhaps one of them had seen Mark—if he had been just as desperate as she was and run out of the gate without her. Portia walked closer, carefully keeping stalls and people between her and the watching guards at the city gate.

Asking around, she was discouraged when none of the vendors had seen Mark. They shook their heads at her, then waved her away when she lingered too long without buying anything. There was limited daylight, and they were already in a disadvantaged location. The last thing they needed was a scrawny orphan interfering with their business.

Portia went to check the other gates again. She could do so by circling the city—all except the harbor gate. No one at the west gate, nor at the north gate, had seen Mark.

She didn't know what to do. It was now close to noon. The sun was hot and high above. She sat down heavily against a tree that backed up against an apple vendor. Her heart hurt. In less than one day, she had lost her gang, who were the only family she could really remember, her home with them, and the orphan she thought of as her little brother. She couldn't remember much of her *other* family, as she thought of them. The one she had been born to. There were odd memories of light flashes, stairs, chains clanking, and a warm fuzzy face looking down on her. She thought the warm face must have belonged to her mother, only because of the safe feeling she associated with it. She couldn't remember any features distinctly. She could only remember a face, and then the loud noises and light flashes. And the trauma of loss afterwards.

Somehow, she had found the gang—or they had found her —giving her a safe place to be. But that was under John, who had been the leader of the gang when she had joined.

John was dead now. Deyelna was in charge, and every-thing had changed. Portia sighed heavily. Three of the four gangs in the city would now attack her on sight. She wasn't sure how long the Lynx would stay friendly, if they were actu-ally friendly at all or just hadn't recognized her.

And not getting attacked was entirely different from being invited to join another gang. Invitations were hard to come by. And precious. They were often the difference between life and death on the streets. Her chance of getting another one was especially low since she had already belonged to a rival gang in the city. Without a gang for protection or a place to live, survival in the city would be difficult.

She stared at the road that led away from the north gate. There were other cities. She had heard of them, especially from the sailors who hung around the harbor gate. Perhaps there was another city friendlier to young orphans. Or at least one without a leader holding a personal grudge against her. She would do whatever it took to blend into the background. Her problems had only started in earnest when Deyelna had realized that Portia could resist her abilities—a rare magical talent. The only other person she knew that had possessed it was now dead, so perhaps that was what Deyelna planned for her as well. Mark did not have it. If Portia was not around, maybe Deyelna would take it easy on him. He had done nothing wrong himself. Portia felt awful even thinking it, but it could be true that Mark would be better off with Portia gone.

And then there was the question of the anti-magicker. And the strange man in black. Something big was going on. Leave it to Deyelna to get involved in that. She was terrifying in her ambition.

The sun was already past its peak. There were only a few hours of daylight left. She glanced at the nearby apple merchant. The woman was middle aged, plump, and looked friendly. Checking her purse, Portia found six coppers. Perhaps that would be enough for some information and some lunch.

"How many apples for a copper?" Portia asked.

The vendor glanced at her, then went back to sorting her piles of apples. "I'll give you a dozen, and a bag, for three coppers."

Portia knew that price was high, but perhaps she could get something more valuable than just apples. She pretended to rummage in her bag to see what money she had to buy some time. "Do you know what lies down that road?" Portia asked, nodding in the direction of the road leading away from the city. The vendor looked up to see where Portia was indicating and then gave a small laugh.

"Ay, a beautiful little hamlet called Holne. Then the royal city past that," the vendor answered.

"Royal city?"

"The big one—Coverack. They got money there, that's for sure. All the vendors want to be working in Holne and get a piece of that action coming from the city. Those schemers ran me and my family out. Now we're here in Valencia," the vendor said, then she spit on the ground, looking disgusted.

"Oh, I'm sorry," Portia said, regretting that she had upset the vendor. She snuck a look at her and saw the woman's cross face and handed over three coppers without argument, even though it was too high a price, because she was too tired to cajole the vendor into a better mood to secure a better one. At least she knew where the road led. The vendor handed her the bag of apples and waved her away.

Portia walked off. She took off her jacket to turn it inside out again, to try to hide as much as possible what she had looked like that day while being chased through the city. She noticed the little Black Cat mark on the collar. She had to get rid of that. She didn't want any sign to show that she was an orphan, much less that she had been a part of a gang.

She pulled out her knife. Picking at the stitching holding the little piece of fabric to her jacket, she managed to get it off without cutting the garment. She pulled the loose threads off and rubbed the spot where the stitches had been to smooth out the holes from the thread. Her jacket was darker where the patch had been. She would just have to hide that part. Reaching down, she grabbed a handful of dirt and rubbed it on the dark spot to disguise it. It was better—the dark spot no longer stood in stark contrast.

Her hand went to the spot on her neck where the gang mark had been placed on her skin. John had done it long ago. She hoped it wasn't magic, just ink. Walking to the well she had seen on the other side of the vendors, she pulled up a bucket of water. She scrubbed at the spot on her neck using the little patch of fabric and water. The only mirror she had was the shiny side of her knife. She rubbed and rubbed, but the spot would not disappear. She closed her eyes and wished with all her might for the mark to fade. Or for it to blend in with the skin somehow. Her neck tingled as she continued scrubbing. She opened her eyes and checked once again to see if the mark was still there. It was not. Her neck was red where she had rubbed, but the small Black Cat symbol was gone. She breathed a sigh of relief.

She considered her options. This was the main road out of Valencia. Due to the sea, there were no other routes, at least none that she knew about. If Mark got out of the city, he would have to come this way. She hoped fervently he did get out—there seemed little good in staying. He knew to avoid the Black Cats, and the other gangs were not good options. Now with this man in black, the city itself was not safe.

But she couldn't stay just outside the city and wait. There was too strong a chance Deyelna would push her gang members outside the gates to search for her, especially at these extended markets. Anywhere there was a market, there was a chance of finding an orphan. Deyelna was smart enough to know that.

Pulling her jacket back on, with the dark spot where the patch had been carefully hidden, she shouldered the bag of apples and walked to the road. She estimated she had a few hours left of daylight and wanted to get as far from the city as possible. There were vendors and farmers on the road making their way home, having either sold all their stock or needing to get home. She joined them on the road. She felt safer if she had someone else in sight. She didn't want to think what she would do when night came. The thought of spending it alone, maybe deep in a forest of unknown creatures, made her stomach hurt. She could not remember sleeping anyplace but the Black Cat den.

After a few hours on the road, her feet throbbed. She felt weak, even after eating several apples. Her coppers would've been better spent on meat or cheese. Even so, she did not want to stop and face the question of where to sleep for the night.

The rumble of wagon wheels coming up behind her caught her attention. She turned to see a large caravan of six wagons, each pulled by two horses. She did not recognize the emblem on the wagon. This must be a trader that went between cities—not every city had a harbor to ship supplies. Some goods had to be transported by wagon.

Two wagons passed her by, then the third one slowed, the driver pulling back on the horses to look at her closely. "Do you want a ride?" he asked.

Portia looked up at the driver. He had an open face with strong laugh lines, shaggy blond hair, and a rough stubble on his chin and jaw. He waited expectantly for her answer. She was exhausted, and her feet hurt like they had never hurt before. But she only had three coppers left. That money needed to go to food. "I don't have any money—at least none I can spare for a ride," she said, wondering if she was doing the right thing.

"Not to worry," he said with a smile. "You don't look like you weigh too much—and the horses won't mind. Get in." He waved to the back of the wagon, stopping the horses completely. Portia hesitated for just a moment, then threw her bag in and climbed up after it. The back of the wagon was empty with only scattered bits of straw on the floor boards along with a pile of blankets that must have covered goods on the way to market.

"Thanks," she said. She sat down awkwardly, leaning against the sideboard of the wagon.

"Make yourself at home," the driver said, motioning towards the blankets. "They're not the cleanest, but we're riding through the night, and it gets a mite bit chilly."

Portia nodded, leaned over, grabbed the pile of blankets, pulled it towards her. She pulled one blanket over herself, then lay down, using the rest of the blankets as a pillow. The driver clicked at the horses, flicked the reins, and directed them to move again. The motion of the wagon felt hypnotic, rocking Portia back and forth.

She thought of Mark. He should have been there with her. She vowed to get enough resources to come back and get him. She would find allies any way she could, she had to, to get him out of that city. Even if Deyelna didn't hate him directly, she still had it out for him because of his association with Portia.

A familiar voice came from ahead. Portia peeked over the side of the wagon—it was Peter. He was dressed in traveling gear. The lead wagon driver had greeted him when passing by, and Peter had replied. Portia had not heard the words— just his voice. He was walking in the same direction they were traveling.

As their wagon approached Peter, Portia ducked down again, pulling the blanket up high over her head, and moved tight against the wagon wall closest to Peter. She hoped that he could not see her at all, or if he did, that her hiding spot looked like a simple pile of blankets. Her breath felt hot under the covers. She counted slowly to a hundred, hoping it was enough for Peter to be long gone. She gave an extra ten just to be sure, then peeked slowly out of the blanket towards the direction they had come from. Peter was a speck in the distance. She held her breath until he disappeared around a turn as the wagon caravan moved on.

She leaned back in relief, then her stomach tightened again in fear—what was Peter doing out there? How had he gotten ahead of her? Had Deyelna sent him on a different task? Portia swallowed uneasily. She had never heard of a gang member being sent outside the city, not for any reason. What was going on with the Black Cats?

A few stars were up in the sky even though the sun had not completely set yet. A shooting star raced across the sky. To calm herself, Portia counted the stars that were out. It helped. She felt her heart slow down. Eventually the motion of the wagon rocked her to sleep.

A GENTLE SHAKE on her shoulder woke her. The driver was leaning over her, holding a canteen. "I forgot to ask you, how far are you going?" he asked, offering her the canteen. She looked at it questioningly. "Ay, don't worry, it's just water. Not that I wouldn't give an arm or a leg for something better," he said with a laugh. He pushed it towards her again—this time she took it. The water tasted fantastic. She forced herself to stop drinking so she wouldn't down the entire thing. She didn't know if he had any other. He noticed and motioned for her to drink again.

"Thanks," she said, feeling embarrassed. She handed back the empty canteen. Portia dug in her bag and pulled out some apples, handing him a few.

He nodded, taking two of the apples in one hand. He took a bite, then looked at her again. "So, how far?" he asked.

She didn't know how to answer. Would it be safe to tell him something? Not that she knew where she was going, just that she was going away from Valencia.

He peered at her. "Are you running away from something?"

"No. No, I'm just... just going on an adventure. I want to see the world outside of Valencia," she said in a rush.

He didn't look like he believed her but didn't press further. He gave her a nod. "I'll wake you when we arrive in Holne. Should be a bit after sunrise. Get some more sleep."

She nodded back, then leaned back, eating her apple. She wondered what this new place would be like. She had never been outside of Valencia before.

6

Portia dreamt of blinding white lights flashing in her face. She tried to avoid them, moving from side to side, but failing miserably. She awoke. The light from the rising sun shone directly on her face. She had a moment of disorientation then remembered where she was—on a wagon headed away from Valencia. She looked up and saw the driver still guiding the horses. She wondered if he had gotten any sleep.

He noticed her looking at him and gave her a wink. "Good, you're awake. Saves me the trouble of getting you roused. We're about to reach Holne. Thought you might want to see it from the top of the hill." He gestured for her to join him on the seat.

Portia sat up, shoved the blankets back in the corner, and joined him. His seat was a few feet higher than the wagon bed, giving a good view of the dew-covered countryside gleaming in the sun. Lush, orderly farm fields gave way to a small hamlet in the distance. Thick thatched roofs topped sturdy stone and brick houses. The town was small but well-made, and well cared for. The lawns and greenery were manicured and neat. She did not see any garbage, as was common on the streets of Valencia.

Portia offered him another apple from her bag, but he waved away. "No more apples; you should be eating better than that anyhow."

She shrugged, abashed. She agreed with him but couldn't do anything about that now. He eyed her but said nothing further.

"After Holne, we're heading out to the next kingdom over. I think that might be a bit too much adventure—more than you're looking for." He laughed. Glancing at her somber face, he stopped laughing. "It's nice enough here," he tried to reassure her.

She nodded, swallowing. She had forgotten there were other kingdoms as well—Haulstatt was the only kingdom she had known. Chatter in the marketplaces of Valencia had spoken of Srubna, Johknovo, and Lusitiana kingdoms, but she knew little of these other lands except their names. It made her feel small.

"Fine with me, I wasn't planning on leaving this kingdom anyhow," she said, hoping he didn't see through her bluff or realize the extent of her ignorance.

"Ay, don't worry, the people here are good." He gave her a gruff pat on the shoulder, trying to be comforting but not that practiced at it.

She stared forward at the town, willing the lump in her

throat to go down. She'd only been on the wagon for one night, but it had felt safe. Now she would have to go off into the unknown again.

The caravan pulled into the central square of the hamlet. The driver pulled up the horses. Leaping down, he held up a hand to help Portia down. She awkwardly took it and jumped down to join him. The driver nodded at the leader of the caravan, who then ducked into a local tavern. The driver turned back to Portia.

"So, where do you plan on going?" he asked.

Portia hesitated. "I'm not sure," she said finally. "Like you said, this place looks nice."

He looked around the town, rubbing the stubble of his beard with one hand. Ducking into the wagon, he grabbed his stick. He waved Portia over to a stretch of bare dirt alongside the cobblestones in the central square.

"Well, if you get bored here, let me show you some things." He smoothed the bare dirt with his foot then started sketching with the stick. "We're here," he jabbed on the ground, "Holne. Up there is Coverack. That's where the bigwigs live—you know, the king and queen and all theirs. Over here," he jabbed again, this time to the west of Coverack, "is the forest of horrors. Don't go there. Not unless you have to, and even then, don't go there."

Portia swallowed. "Why?"

Just then, the caravan leader came out of the tavern, walked to them, and tapped the driver on the shoulder and nodded; it was time for them to get going.

The driver gave Portia a rueful look. "Wish I had time to

explain more. Perhaps someone here can tell you. But trust me on this one."

Portia felt fear run up her spine as the driver leapt back onto the wagon. They were leaving. She checked that she had her bag. He looked at her, then rummaged around in his jacket, and pulled out a few coins. Leaning down, he dropped them into Portia's bag. "It's not much. Go get something to eat besides apples, and perhaps some better clothes." The caravan lead pulled away, the second wagon falling in the line. The driver clicked at his horses to join in turn before Portia had a chance to thank him.

She looked down at her clothes—they were torn and dirty. All the fighting yesterday had damaged them beyond repair. There were rips from when other orphans had grabbed her, trying to keep her from escaping, as well as cuts from at least one knife. She looked around at the few people out and about in the early morning sunshine. They were well-dressed, clean. The fabrics of their clothes were fine linens, even a few velvets and silks. No one had torn clothes. Nor dirty ones. She did not fit in. She brushed the dirt from the wagon off her breeches and jacket. The breeches made her feel even more self-conscious. All the women she had seen here wore kirtles. Could the style of clothing be that much different just one town over?

Glancing around the town square, she saw a clothier shop a few storefronts down from the tavern. She checked her bag for the coins the driver had left her—five silver. It was more money than she'd ever seen before, at least in her own hands, but she feared it was not enough to buy the fine clothes she saw around her. She'd have to make do with what she could afford and be grateful at that. She needed money for food as well.

She squared her shoulders, lifting her head high. She strode down to the clothier shop, opened the door, and entered. She struggled to see in the dim interior as her eyes adjusted. The walls were lined with bolts of beautiful fabrics. Shelves held fine clothes. Several kirtles hung from hangers waiting to be claimed by customers. There didn't appear to be anybody in the shop.

"Goodness! You're a fright. Who would let you out of the house like that?" A voice came from behind her, startling her. The shopkeeper emerged from behind a shelf of fabric bolts and walked closer to get a better look at Portia. She looked her up and down but did not ask her to leave. Portia stood there awkwardly. She wished the shopkeeper would stop staring. When a moment went by and it was clear she was not going to be tossed out, Portia walked to the nearest rack of fabric. "No, no—don't touch those," the shopkeeper said, rushing towards her, blocking her hands from the fine material, "Not until you've cleaned yourself up anyhow."

Portia looked at her questioningly. The shopkeeper grabbed her by the arm and pulled her towards the rear of the store. They passed through the back room that had even more fabric rolls and a large sink discolored from fabric dye. The shopkeeper grabbed a bar of soap from the sink while still gripping Portia's arm tightly, then continued to a rear door.

She pulled Portia outside into a lush backyard. A small well stood twenty feet away in the middle of a large green lawn. It was surrounded by a low stone circular wall and was covered by a structure with pulleys and rope. The entire thing was roofed with cedar shake. A fence surrounded the yard, running around tall trees that edged the yard. This yard could have been in the middle of the woods for not a glimpse could be seen of any neighboring house.

"Wash yourself here," the shopkeeper said, tossing Portia the bar of soap. Portia caught it with both hands. "There are washing cloths in the little hutch next to the bucket," the shopkeeper said, nodding at the tiny structure the bucket rested on, next to the stone wall surrounding the well. She then turned with a swirl and went back into the shop. Portia could not figure out how old the shopkeeper was. She appeared young, and old at the same time. Her hair at first looked blonde in the shop but then seemed to turn gray in the light outside. When Portia had tried to look closer, it was blonde again.

Portia tossed the bucket into the well. It landed with a splash. She pulled up the fresh, clean water, then drank heavily. The water was cold and refreshing. Her fingers and toes tingled in an odd way, but the water tasted so good that she ignored the unusual sensation and took another drink.

She grabbed one of the cloths from the hutch. Even it was a fine linen—rough but pleasing. This town must be well-off indeed if even their cleaning rags were so wonderful. She looked around, feeling uncomfortable in the open like this. Alone. She usually bathed, when she had that luxury, in the harbor with the other Black Cats. There was little privacy, true, but there had been safety in numbers. One or more Black Cats could keep an eye out for other orphan gangs, while the rest took their turn in the muddy water of the harbor. Here, there was no one else but her.

She peered around the yard. There was not another person to be seen. Even so, she gritted her teeth with anxiety at being caught. She undressed in a rush. Dipping the wash-cloth in the clean water of the bucket, she washed as quickly as she could. Dirt ran down her arms and legs, soaking the grass around the well. Throwing the bucket down for another load of water, she drew it back up again and poured it over her head, soaping her hair as best she could. One final rinse more and she was done. Goosebumps rose on her arms even while standing in the full sunlight. She reached for her dirty clothes, distasteful as they were.

"Stop." The shopkeeper's voice rang out over her shoulder. "You'll just get dirty again." The shopkeeper walked quickly towards her, her arms holding out a wide expanse of clean white fabric. She reached Portia, wrapping the crisp cloth around her. "Dry off with this. Wrap it around yourself when you're done and come inside. Leave those rags out here. I'll deal with them later." The shopkeeper returned inside, not waiting to see if Portia obeyed. Portia watched her go, then bent down, fished the coins from her jacket where she had stashed them, and grabbed her bag. She didn't know if she had enough silver for shoes too, so took a hold of her boots as well. She followed the shopkeeper inside.

The shopkeeper waved her into a small dressing room that

Portia did not remember seeing when she first came in the shop. The shopkeeper snapped the curtain shut behind Portia. The dressing room only had a small stool and several hooks on the wall. There were no clothes inside of it.

"Are there any colors you prefer?" the shopkeeper's voice rang out over the curtain.

"Red and black, ma'am." Portia had always liked red, but it was too bright a color for a thief. If she was going to have a new life like she wanted, and hopefully not as a thief, she could at least wear her favorite colors.

"Don't 'ma'am' me," tisked the shopkeeper. "My name is Alice. Call me that."

"Okay... Alice." Portia felt uncomfortable using the woman's first name.

"Good girl. Now let me see what I can find for you." A moment later, a beautiful set of clothes—a deep red and black kirtle, black breaches, and a fine white linen shirt—were thrust around the curtain. "See how these fit you. They look like your size."

Portia took the outfit in her hands. The wool of the breeches and kirtle felt smooth. It was densely woven, finer than any wool she'd ever had. She pulled on the linen shirt and breeches but wasn't sure how to lace the long woolen kirtle. She emerged from the dressing room.

Alice nodded in satisfaction. "Much better." She stepped forward, motioned for Portia to come closer. Alice grabbed the laces of the kirtle and pulled them tight, giving them a good tie. She pushed Portia towards a polished metal mirror. The outfit hugged her form perfectly. Except for her tousled wet hair, she looked more like one of the ladies outside in the square than an orphan on the run.

Portia was surprised at how different she looked. "This is much nicer... I mean, I don't know if I can afford this," Portia said, stuttering. She regretted trying them on to begin with before asking the price. She didn't want a scene, such as what would happen if she was thrown out of the shop.

"Four silver," Alice replied briskly. She gave Portia's shoulders a little squeeze, nodded at her in the mirror. "Yes, this will do indeed."

Four silver? That was all? She breathed a sigh of relief. She couldn't believe her luck. Somehow, it didn't seem right the clothes were so cheap. "That is all you want for them? Really?"

"Yes, girl. You're in luck—you chose colors that are not popular," the seamstress said, turning from Portia to straighten what already seemed to be straight stacks of clothes. "This way, I get them off my shelves, and you get something to wear."

Portia didn't quite believe her but didn't want to argue. Looking at her reflection in the mirror, she couldn't believe it was really her. She looked like a young woman, not a dirty orphan from the streets. She wanted to own these beautiful clothes. And she'd still have money left for food. Before Alice could change her mind, she grabbed the coins from her bag and handed over four silver pieces.

"Thank you," Portia said.

"No worries, no worries, off you go," Alice said, waving Portia towards the door.

Portia hesitated. "Should I go and get my old clothes from the back?" She motioned to the backyard.

"No, no. Leave them be—I'll take care of it. Here," Alice said, turning to Portia, pushing a bone comb into her hands. "A gift for you. It looks like you need it." She gave her a warm smile, softening the comment.

Portia nodded, taking the comb. She shoved it into her bag while returning the shopkeeper's smile. "Thank you again."

Exiting the shop, the sun was high in the sky. Portia's stomach rumbled, reminding her that she had only eaten apples since yesterday. The water from the well could only satisfy her so much. She needed to eat. She spotted the same tavern the caravan had stopped in front of earlier that morning. She wasn't sure what the customs here were for eating in alehouses, but there didn't appear to be a market that day. She would have to face the public eatery if she wanted lunch.

Entering the tavern, the noise and smells of the packed alehouse washed over her, overwhelming her. She forced herself to continue inside. Every table and booth was full of people. She had not noticed so many citizens about in town, so she had not expected them here now. She stood surveying the room, unsure what to do. Perhaps she should come back later.

Before she could exit, a bartender stepped up in front of her, a white apron wrapped around his slender body, only his thinning hair betraying his age. "Can I help you?"

"I had wanted to eat, but there aren't any seats," she replied.

"Not out here, true. I think I can scrounge one up for you in back. We've got some private booths—don't mind sharing, do you?" he asked, walking to the back, not waiting to hear her response.

"No, of course not," she said, doubting he could hear her over the din of the loud voices in the open room. She felt for her dagger in case it was a trap. The noise of the room set her nerves on edge.

He opened a door and leaned in. "The tavern is crowded. Do you mind if someone joins you?"

Portia could not hear the response, but the bartender opened the door further and ushered her in. It was a tiny room with one table in it surrounded by benches topped with soft cushions. Two people sat at the table—a young boy of about ten years old, with wild brown hair, and an older woman wearing robes of silver and blue. They looked up and smiled at Portia and the bartender. Portia smiled back at them. The bartender motioned her inside. Portia slid onto the bench closest to the door.

"So, beef is ten coppers, chicken is five, ale included in both. What can I get for you?" the bartender asked, looking expectantly at all three of them.

The woman waved his question away. "We've already ordered."

Portia checked her purse. She didn't want to spend her last silver coin, and she only had three coppers left besides that. She looked at the bartender, trying to look sweet and demur. "How about food only, for three coppers?"

The bartender considered her offer. Portia gave him a small smile. Finally, he nodded. "Sure. I'll send the maid back with that." Portia handed over her coins to him. He pocketed them then shut the door, leaving the three of them alone in the room together.

The young boy stared at Portia until the older woman nudged him to stop. He picked up a fork and played with it, sneaking glances at Portia. The older woman gave him another look but didn't criticize him further. She looked to Portia. "My name is Professor Hilda Griffiths, and this young man is Randall." When Portia only nodded, the older woman prompted further, "What is your name, young lady?"

"Portia, ma'am."

Professor Hilda laughed at that. "No 'ma'am,' please. I feel like I am still your age—being called ma'am ruins that all. Call me Hilda, Professor Griffiths, or just Professor if you must give me a title."

Portia felt her cheeks go red. She wasn't used to speaking to adults, at least those so well-off as this one. She wasn't sure what a professor was. "Okay... Professor."

"So, are you local?" Hilda asked Portia.

"No, I'm just visiting."

Randall looked at Portia. "Us too. Are you going to the Academy?" He kicked a little in excitement, bouncing up and down on his seat slightly. Hilda gave him a stern look. He stopped bouncing.

"Academy?" Portia asked.

Their conversation was interrupted by the door opening. A waitress entered, carrying three wooden bowls of sop and chicken in one arm, and three mugs of ale in the other. She laid the meal out in front of the guests. Portia motioned the glass away, but the waitress just patted her on the arm. "No worries dear; it's taken care of."

"But I can't—"

The waitress interrupted her. "He's got it," she said, motioning with her head to the front of the tavern where the bartender was working.

Portia reluctantly took the glass. The ale looked delicious, but she didn't want to have to part with silver to pay for it. The waitress gave her a reassuring look and exited, shutting the door on the three diners.

Portia took a bite of the food and realized how ravenous she was. She took another bite before she had even finished chewing the first one. It tasted so good. She knew she was eating too fast and drawing the looks of Hilda and Randall, but she couldn't help it. She looked down while she ate, refusing to meet their eyes.

All too soon, her bowl was empty. She scraped her spoon along it, getting the last of the liquid. Her stomach rumbled for more food. She looked up to see Randall and Hilda only halfway through their meals. Hilda politely did not look at her or censure her glances at their food. Portia grabbed her mug of ale and drank half of it, willing her stomach to be satisfied with that. It worked, and she was able to lean back and relax, closing her eyes. Her ravenous desire for food was satisfied for the moment.

"The Magic Academy," Hilda said quietly.

Portia opened her eyes and looked at Hilda. "What?"

"The school, you know, the one where they teach magic," Randall said. "I'm going to go there."

Hilda raised her eyebrows at him. "We hope. There is still the test."

"I'm going to pass the test. I've been training my whole life." Randall said, his voice rising in pitch. Hilda sighed but did not say anything else.

Portia looked back and forth between the two of them in confusion. "You can't teach magic. Either you have it, or you don't."

"That's not true!" Randall said. "You're wrong."

"Randall, let's not be rude," Patricia said, patting his arm. "Besides, she's not entirely wrong. It's true that some people are born with it. You know that."

Randall nodded.

Hilda turned her attention to Portia. "There are three types of magic users. Yes, some people are born with an innate ability. But they also can be taught how to control their magic and how to strengthen it. That is the most common type of magic. The second kind have slightly more extensive abilities. They can study an entire tree of magic. For instance, they could be able to use all magic related to air."

"That's me," Randall said.

"You can do all magic related to air?" Portia asked, incredulous.

Randall cupped his hands together in the shape of a ball, muttering under his breath and focusing his eyes on the center of his hands. A small ball of whirling air formed above his palms, getting stronger. Portia felt her hair moving in the breeze it created.

"Stop showing off," Hilda said, grabbing the napkins off the table before they flew off in the wind. "Randall has the ability for air—we don't know yet if he has the ability for the entire magical tree of air skills."

Randall stopped concentrating on the ball of air, letting it dissolve. "I do. Just wait and see." He jutted his chin out and crossed his arms on his chest.

Portia had tried to take this all in. She had no idea there was a place you could go to learn magic. And this boy was going to attend. It didn't seem fair. She knew lots of orphans with magical abilities, but they were lucky if they survived to adulthood. She stared at Randall. His cheeks were full, flushed red with food and ale, and his clothing looked new. She doubted he had ever missed a meal in his life. A bitter taste flooded her mouth.

"You're very lucky," she said, trying to be gracious.

"Do you have magic?" Randall asked, but didn't wait for a reply. "If you have magic, you can take the test too. Anyone can."

Portia stared at Randall in disbelief. Hilda saw the look on her face. "It's true. The King decreed that anyone with ability should be trained. It's safer for the kingdom that way."

"How... how do you get to take the test?" Portia asked.

"It's given twice a year in Coverack," Hilda said. "Sign up for one of the testing sessions."

"You just show up?"

"You have to send a letter reserving your spot. There is a registration process. It's not too onerous," Hilda said, pushing her plate away and gathering her bags. She paused, looked up. "The King has decreed instructions posted in every town. I'm surprised you don't know this."

The door to the private booth opened and a man with a hat and beard poked his head in. "The caravan is leaving in five, please be outside. I'm not allowed to wait for anybody." He disappeared just as quickly, shutting the door behind himself.

Hilda looked at Portia. "Sorry, dear, that was our driver. Randall, finish up; we have to go if you want to take that test."

Randall shoved the rest of his meal in his mouth. Portia didn't think he chewed once before swallowing it all.

Hilda slid out between the benches and the table, moving towards the door, followed closely by Randall. They exited the private booth. Hilda was almost lost in the crowd before Portia realized she hadn't told her about the third magic user type. She leapt up to follow after the professor and her young charge. Portia pushed through the crowd and caught up to Hilda. She grabbed her arm, stopping her. "Wait, what is the third magic type?"

"Why dear, it's Jack of Magic. It's someone who can use any type of magic," Hilda said, patting Portia's hand, then leaning in conspiratorially. "Personally, I think it's a myth, but that's neither here nor there." Hilda straightened up again, turned to see Randall running off to the exit. "I do so hate to be rude, but we really must go." Hilda quickly followed the boy out the door.

Portia stood in the crowded alehouse. *Myth?* That couldn't be her, could it? Maybe she was just lucky and all her magic was the same magic tree, whatever a magic tree was.

A man tried to get past her, but there was so little room in the crowded tavern that he knocked her into a table with three workmen around it. She apologized to the surprised men, flustered, then headed quickly for the exit. She emerged just as a caravan of carriages was pulling out of the square. Randall spied her from inside one of them and waved at her as they drove past.

Portia wished with all her heart she was in that carriage too being taken to Coverack.

She allowed herself a moment to feel sorry for herself as she watched the carriages drive away. Then she shook herself. She needed to concentrate on surviving.

And maybe she could go to that Academy, even if she didn't ride a carriage there like Randall did. She just had to find a way to get to Coverack.

Looking around the square, she didn't see any other wagons or carriages. She felt her single silver coin. It would be unwise to spend her last money on a ride in any event. She sighed then turned towards the road to Coverack. A figure in a dark blue jacket caught the corner of her eye. It looked familiar. Turning, she saw Peter walking towards her. She cursed—she had forgotten about him on the road.

She panicked and ducked back into the entryway of a butcher shop. Crowded patrons pushed back at her.

Worse yet, her quick motion had attracted Peter's attention. He ran towards her just as the patrons were shoving her back out of the butcher shop. She ran towards the road, but Peter was faster and caught up to her, grabbing her arm and pulling her to a halt.

"Leave me alone!" she yelled at him, trying to attract attention.

"Quiet!" he hissed at her, pulling her close. "Don't make a scene."

"Why not?" she said, yanking at her arm, trying to escape.

"Because if you do, it'll hurt Mark." He yanked her back. "A lot."

She stopped struggling, turned to stare at him. "I don't believe you." She glared at him, trying to see if he was lying. It was standard procedure to say anything that was needed to control victims. More than likely, the Black Cats had not captured Mark. She hoped.

"I don't care if you believe me or not," Peter said, irritated at her belligerence. "You're coming back with me."

"Why? Deyelna wanted to get rid of me. I'm gone. Why drag me back?"

"Because you ruined her plans. Now she's angry," Peter said with a grimace. "She's going to take it out of your hide."

"She is, or is her little errand boy going to do it for her?" Portia asked, angry at Peter's blind obedience to Deyelna.

"Enough!" he said. He looked around the square to see if anyone was watching. A woman and her daughter had been staring but quickly looked away and walked down the street away from them when Peter focused his gaze on them. There was no one else in the square. "I should be at home reading.

Instead, I'm sent on this stupid task of retrieving you. I am already fed up. Don't make it worse."

Portia just got angrier. Peter was worried about his reading? And all this for Deyelna, with her insatiable appetite for control? Portia summoned all her energy. She poured it into creating a blinding field of light on her skin, imitating Mark's magic. Peter yelped, turned away from her, and fell, letting go of her arm. Portia ran down the street.

She passed the far corner of the square and turned onto the road. Peter scrambled to his feet behind her. She turned and saw two of him; he was using his magic. She cursed and veered left then right, to avoid her pursuers.

The Peters gained on her. She felt her stomach complain. The food in it jostled with each step. She felt nauseous. She kept running, hoping to lose the Peters before she was sick.

One of them came up on her left side while the second was falling behind. Desperate, she hoped the Peter to her left was the duplicate—one that he could send running faster than he could in real life. An abandoned wagon wheel in the road forced her to veer towards it instead of right. If it was the duplicate Peter, she should be able to run right through it.

But it was the real Peter. They collided and tumbled to the ground.

Portia rolled to her back, her feet up defensively. Peter tried to pin her down, but she was too fast and kicked him in the groin with all her strength. He grunted, doubled over. She kicked him in the chest, knocking him over to lay in the road, moaning. She swung her bag—which still had half a dozen apples in it—at his head as hard as she could. His moan silenced.

She stood, panting, waiting for him to get up, but he never did. Coming closer, she could see he was breathing, but he was out cold.

She leaned over him and pulled out her dagger.

7

Peter's breathing was even. His pale skin had a sheen of sweat on it. She was so close she could smell the scent of leather and the musk he always used.

She held her dagger over his chest, ready to plunge it into his heart. Her arms trembled. She had never killed anybody. She had never even really hurt anybody. A shiver of revulsion passed up her spine and across her skull as she thought of the blade slicing through his flesh and landing deep in his heart. Bile rose in her throat.

She fought with herself for a minute, then threw her dagger to the side with a curse. It was probably a mistake, but she would not start butchering people now. She could not do it.

But she needed to get away from him. On impulse, she raised her right foot and slammed it down on his big toe. She heard the crunch of a bone breaking, but Peter didn't move. Maybe that would slow him down enough.

She retrieved her dagger and put it back into its sheath. Looking around the square, she didn't see anyone. She thought she saw the curtain of the clothier fall shut but told herself it was just her imagination. Portia jogged onto the road to Coverack, leaving Peter in the dust behind her.

HER JOGGING TURNED into walking soon after. She spent the next several hours trudging along the road, continually checking behind her to see if Peter was coming. She wondered if that was worse than killing him would have been. Then she shook her head no. She would never find a place in this kingdom if she became a murderer.

Or maybe she was just weak and just couldn't do what needed to be done. She refused to believe that.

The road was quiet. She wished there was some traffic, even if it brought the risk of Peter hitching a ride. Being alone felt unfamiliar. In the city, there were always other people about. Voices were a constant presence in her life until now, even if heard through a wall. Here, there was nothing but the sound of crickets and birds from the nearby forest. Thankfully, the road didn't run directly through the forest—it was dark and foreboding. It was bad enough that the road ran along the forest the entire way. Every time she checked for Peter, she also checked the trees, but for what, she didn't know.

The sun was glaring in her eyes as it drew closer to the horizon. She didn't want to be on the road alone after dark.

Nor did she really want to be in the forest. She decided the edge of the forest would be safer than venturing too far in, and still safer than being visible from the road.

Scanning the dark wood, she noticed a group of five trees up ahead. They appeared taller than the rest but were heavily foliaged, especially in the upper branches. It would be hard for anyone to see her there from the road. They would've had to been looking for her, and even then, would most likely miss her.

She looked up the tallest of the five trees. It was the one furthest from the road. Her stomach grew queasy at the height. She told herself to pretend it was a warehouse building with a nice ladder up the side, and a safe flat roof waiting for her on top. She jumped to grab the lowest branch and pulled herself up. She climbed halfway up the tree, going from branch to branch until there was an unusually large gap between the branches which stopped her from climbing higher. Looking around below her and towards the road, Portia decided she wasn't high enough. She could easily see the road, which meant anyone on the road could easily see her.

Looking up the tree again, she saw a thick branch ten feet above her. She reached for where she normally had her rope, but it was not there. She had lost the last of it that night in the warehouse with Mark. Gazing at the rough bark under her fingers, she wished it was a ladder up the tree. She imagined the ladder rungs spaced evenly a foot apart going up the tree. She felt a tingle in her neck and in her fingertips. Light flickered on the edge of her vision from her hands onto the tree. As she watched, the bark pushed out from the tree under her into the shape of a ladder leading up. The tree groaned, and the bark creaked, but nothing broke off or gave way. Portia had never seen anything like this before. Unconsciously she held her breath until she realized she was getting dizzy and then gasped in some air. The growth of the tree had slowed when she had stopped breathing. It picked up its pace once again, then halted, leaving a wood ladder leading up ten feet to the next branches. It amazed Portia. She also felt a little guilty—she hoped she hadn't hurt the tree.

Cautiously, she gripped the first rung on the wood ladder and pulled. It held fast. She tested the next rung with her other hand and found the same result. Gingerly, she pulled herself up and put her right foot on the lowest rung. Slowly, she put her weight on it. It did not give. She hopped on it, trying to make it break or at least seeing how much force it would take to make a break, but again it did not give way. She looked up one last time and made a leap of faith. She scrambled up the rest of the ladder as fast as she could, counting on it being the same as the bottom rung she had already tested. Reaching the branches above the bare spot on the tree, she climbed into them with a sense of relief. She never heard of magic working like that on a living thing before.

She found a crook in the branches where two branches grew away from the tree nearly parallel to each other, leaving a nest-like place for her to sit. She perched there, leaning against the main trunk. She wished she had some rope to tie herself in. She wrapped her bag strap around herself and the trunk. It helped but would not be enough to keep her from falling if she relaxed into a deep sleep. And she needed sleep more than anything else.

Looking at the surrounding branches, she imagined them coming in to give her a hug. She felt the familiar tingle down the back of her spine. Soon after, the branches leaned in towards her, gingerly at first, then picking up speed. In a moment, the branches wrapped her in a cocoon of thin branches and leaves, wrapping around her body and only leaving her face exposed. She let herself relax slowly, bit by bit, testing her makeshift bed. It felt solid. She even shook it with her arms and legs, rattling the leaves and sending a few falling to the ground. It did not give. She exhaled with relief. She could sleep.

The air cooled as the sun set. Portia shivered. She willed the branches to tuck even closer to her body, which they quickly obliged. The leaves on the branches holding her tight insulated her enough to stop her shivering. She closed her eyes.

THE WORLD RUMBLED AND SHOOK. A loud keening rang out in the night. Slowly, a crack worked its way from the ground, zigzagging up through the sky and across the heavens above. The rumbling and shaking increased in intensity, moving the trees back and forth to the point of breaking. The keening noise rose in pitch. Slowly, the halves of the heavens pulled apart in jerks and starts until a black void, darker than the darkest patch of the night sky, filled the space between the two halves of heaven. It was empty of everything—of stars, of glowing light, of anything in nature.

Portia started awake with a jerk. Her heart was racing. She gripped the tree tightly until she felt her heart slow, until her pulse no longer throbbed in her neck.

The forest was quiet around her. She held her breath until she heard the faint cry of an owl. Slowly, she could make out other forest noises. She felt reassured that everything was all right. If something was coming, surely the animals in the woods would know.

The sun was rising in the east, tinging the sky pink. Rather than try to get more sleep, she thought it would be best to get an early start on the road. She pulled out an apple and ate it, waiting for the sun to chase away more of the darkness. Willing the branches back to their natural place, she released herself and then climbed down the tree.

When she got to the bottom, she looked up at the ladder she had created. She put a palm on the trunk, closed her eyes, and told it, *Thank you for your help. I'm sorry if it hurt.* She felt bad for how she had changed it. Portia's hand tingled where it touched the tree. She opened her eyes, looked up, and gasped—the ladder slowly receded back into the tree, leaving not a single mark on the trunk. She backed away, not sure what was going on. She wished at that moment John was still alive. He'd been the closest thing to a teacher she had ever had. If it wasn't for him, she never would have survived her first years as an orphan in Valencia.

She returned to the road, turning towards Coverack. After an hour, the creak of wagon wheels behind her alerted her to traffic on the road. She turned and saw a beautiful carriage with the same insignia as the royal ship in the harbor of Valencia. She backed away from the road at the behest of the driver who waved her back with his whip. He looked imperious and didn't turn towards her as they drove by, his head held high and straightforward. The carriage was beautiful, with gold paint and curving woodwork. It was fully enclosed, the windows covered with curtains. Portia couldn't see who was inside. She watched it go by in awe. Four guards on horseback followed closely, holding long pikes in readiness, swords strapped to their sides.

She followed, watching the carriage disappear in the distance ahead of her. Hopefully, this meant she wasn't far from the city. She should have asked how far Coverack was from Holne. Her stomach rumbled, making her wonder if she shouldn't have tried to catch a rabbit or something from the forest last night.

Thoughts of food consumed her. She stared at the ground, thinking of rabbit stew when a voice startled her from her daydreams.

"Well, isn't that a pretty one?" A man stood in the road ahead of her. Portia was furious at herself for not paying attention. She should have been looking around. The man had dirty breeches and even dirtier hair. He was missing a front tooth. She could tell because he gave her a leering smile while he looked her up and down, his arms crossed.

"That she is, that she is," a voice came from behind her. Portia whirled around to see another man, equally disgusting, standing behind her. She backed away from the road, trying to see both men at once instead of being trapped between them.

"Now, now… no need to be afraid, sweetie," the first man said, breathing heavily and walking towards her. "We've just been a little robbed this morning with only the royal carriage coming through and more guards than we want to mess with. But it's all better now. You've come here. And now we can party." He gave her a sickly smile she feared was meant to reassure her. It did not.

The second man laughed at that. "Party." He had a leering grin to match the first man. Portia did not want to know what sort of party they had in mind. She used Mark's magic to create bright lights on her skin, but she wasn't close enough to truly blind them, only to knock out their vision for a few minutes. When they shut their eyes and hissed, she bolted away around the first man to run further down the road then veered off into the forest to hide behind a tree. She created a duplicate of herself and sent it down the road towards Coverack. She thought better, and reversed the duplicate's course, sending it back down the road from the way she had come, past the men and back towards Holne. She did not want these men running in the same direction she was going.

She stopped the duplicate a bit down the road by having it trip and fall. It was still in view of the men. Her timing was perfect. By the time the duplicate stood again, the men's vision cleared, and they spied it. She sent the duplicate running down the road again, leading both men away from her. When they were out of sight, she walked back on the road towards Coverack, keeping further to the side this time. She wanted to have a clear escape path to the forest in case any other bandits were out and about. It was exhausting, but she concentrated on keeping the duplicate running behind her, all the while looking out around herself and walking forward. After half an hour, she figured they were far enough away—she let go of the magic holding the duplicate in existence and breathed out a tired sigh.

Soon after, the city of Coverack appeared in the distance. It was a jewel of red and white stone buildings rising from the fields. It sat next to the mountains to the south. Beyond it, she could see the blue of the sea. A dark castle with many tall towers sat at the far side. The city was as beautiful as Holne but twenty times its size, if not more. The main gate was three times the width of the main gate for Valencia and twice as tall. A dozen guards patrolled outside it, plus additional guards walked in the inner courtyard. This was a rich city. Even the peasants who walked in and out of the gates looked as well-to-do as the merchants in Valencia. Portia was in awe.

Portia got in line to enter the city. She didn't have any merchandise or obvious reason to enter the city. She scanned her brain, trying to come up with a story, but was drawing a blank. She walked closely behind a wagon full of pumpkins, hoping the guard would mistake her for being part of the farmer's group. To her surprise, the guard barely looked at her. He barely looked at anybody in fact, just waved everyone through. She wondered about that. How could they be so sure the people walking through the gates were good for the city? Did they have security measures she didn't know about?

Entering the courtyard just inside the gate, Portia looked

around. She had no idea where the tests were held for the Magic Academy or how to sign up for them. She needed more information. She spied a pastry stall on the far side of the square and made her way over to it. The pastry seller didn't even try to shortchange her. This was definitely a different town than Valencia.

Buying her breakfast, she turned to watch the people in the courtyard and picked out conversing groups she might go and overhear. She spied a group of young men unloading produce near a set of stopped carriages from whence travelers unloaded—their cloaks and bags gave away that they had come from a great distance. It seemed likely that some of them were coming here for the test for the Magic Academy. Portia made her way over to the travelers. She wanted to learn more. She leaned against a tree nearby and tried to be invisible as she finished the last of her pastry.

"Made it just in time," one young woman said, adjusting her cloak after stepping down from a carriage. "They need to do something about those bandits."

"Agreed," another young woman said. This young woman accepted a bag from the carriage footman and looked around the square. She spied the young men unloading produce behind her and gave them a shy smile.

"Stop," whined the first young woman. "We are here for magic, that's all." The second young woman gave her an irritated look.

A matron exited the carriage. She scowled when she saw the young men nearby and the distracted looks of her charges. She waved at the girls to grab their bags and ushered them towards a building nearby with a hanging sign of a rooster over its doorway. Portia guessed it was an inn. The matron scolded her charges. "Focus, girls. Do not expect another chance at this—it cost your parents a pretty penny to get you here for this one. They won't have the coin for another try in six months."

Portia continued around the square listening to other conversations. It turned out that the test started tomorrow, and the town was filling with applicants eager to prove their case that they belonged at the Academy. All the applicants looked so young—younger than her, and younger than Mark even. She wondered if there was an age requirement. But she couldn't worry about that now. She had no other plans. She couldn't go back to Valencia, not with Deyelna and the rest of the city's gangs after her.

Since the tests started tomorrow, Portia hoped she would still have time to take the test. No one had spoken of how they had gotten their spot, but she did learn where the Magic Academy was. It was up the hill, a third of the way to the castle. She went there to plead her case.

As she approached the Academy, its clean lines impressed her. There was more than one building, but it was clear they were all together because they were the only buildings in the city made of blue stone. She had never seen buildings that color before. They sparkled with magic—it was the only way they could look the way they did. Her stomach tightened when she looked at them, and she felt a strong pull. Something was telling her this was the place she needed to be.

She stepped onto the campus and felt a tingle go all over

her body. It was the same sensation as stepping into the shower, but she could not see any water or any other reason for it. She was dry. But she did not let the sensation stop her, especially since she felt no force pushing against her. She made her way to the main building that was front and center of the drive up.

There were two guardsmen on the outside of the building, dressed in blue livery. They looked a little surprised to see her, she could tell, by the tightening of their eyes. Did they not expect any visitors the day before the test? But again, they did not stop her. Instead, they wordlessly nodded at her then opened the front doors in unison. She nodded back, entering the building.

The inside was dark when she had first looked in but grew gradually lighter and lighter when she entered. She could not see the light source. It seemed to glow directly from the walls and ceiling. The entry was empty—and gigantic. There was nothing in it to absorb the sound, so her footsteps echoed and reverberated back at her. She stopped in the entry's middle and looked at the two staircases arching both left and right up to a tall landing in front of her and then away to both sides again. She could see nothing further up there. There was no one around.

"Hello?" she called out tentatively. No one answered. Would it be impertinent for her to go exploring to find some-one? No one had told her she could not be here, but she would hate to lose her chance to test by breaking some unknown rule. "Hello?" she called out again.

A shimmering column formed in the entryway's center,

coalescing into the image of an old woman dressed in long robes. The woman was slightly see-through, so Portia knew she was not really there. She wondered where the woman was if this was a duplicate. The woman looked at her assessingly. She nodded slowly, then addressed Portia. "How may I help you?"

Portia swallowed, nervous. "I'm here to take the test. I have magic..." Portia trailed off. She didn't know what argument to use, only that the tests were open if you had magical ability.

The old woman held up her hand to stop Portia from speaking further. "Have you an invitation?" she asked. Portia shook her head no. "Then you may not test. All invitations for this cycle have gone out."

"How do you get an invitation?"

"By asking for one by letter or in person before rolls close," the old woman said. "Rolls closed yesterday for the session. Come back in five months and two weeks and register for the testing that shall begin in six months hence. You may test then."

"But I'm here now. Surely there is a way to fit one more in?" Portia asked, her face flushed red with the shameful feeling she was begging.

"There is not. This is how it has always been and how it will always be. Return as I have told you." The old woman looked down after speaking. Her image shimmered away into nothing.

Portia stared now at the opposite side of the entryway through where the old woman had been. "Wait, wait!" she called. She turned in a panic, trying to find anybody to speak to. There was no one. The doors behind her opened, and she saw the two men in livery waiting for her to exit. She swallowed and straightened her shoulders, walking out with her head up. She wondered how much they had heard.

Leaving the Academy grounds was painful. She was at a loss of what to do. She had to survive in this town for six months, or go elsewhere. Once again, she was homeless—and now on the run from Deyelna and her minion, Peter, and possibly others.

Looking down at what she could see of the city from the Academy, she spied an area that was more rundown than the rest of the town. There were wooden planks nailed to buildings in a half effort to repair roofs, crumbling plaster walls on many buildings, and trash on the streets. It was the first trash she had seen in the entire city. It looked more like Valencia than any other place in the city. She thought she should go there since she might blend in better.

Portia spied a washing woman coming her way lugging a large basket of laundry. She intercepted her and asked what the name of the rundown district was. The washerwoman replied that it was the Warrens while also warning her away from it. Portia nodded her thanks and waited for the kind woman to continue on her way before she headed directly towards the area the woman had cautioned her about.

The Warrens were just as she expected—vagrants on the streets, rough-looking fellows, and women who leered at her as much as they did the men. It was familiar to her, and for that alone it felt comforting. She walked several blocks, trying to find a place that was a likely gang house.

Portia felt a hand on her side and instinctively grabbed it with her left. She realized the hand was on her dagger, trying to steal it. While still hanging on the offending appendage, she whirled to face a gritty young man. He pulled back on his hand, giving her a forced smile. She did not let go. His smile faltered. He straightened, and because she still gripped his hand, ended up pulling her closer.

He smirked. "Such a pretty dagger belongs with someone like me, don't you think?" he asked.

"No," she said, gritting her teeth.

He tried to shake his hand free. "Well, if you don't think so, why are you still holding on to my hand? Are you sweet on me, dearest?" he asked, looking pointedly at his hand.

"Because," she said, removing his hand from her dagger with her left while her right grabbed the hilt and pulled the blade from its sheath, "I thought you might want to see its usefulness." She swung the dagger out towards the man, zigzagging left and right with its tip close to his body. She stood back a moment. Slowly, his tunic and shirt fell in shreds to the ground. He looked down incredulously. There was not a mark on his body. She had neatly sliced his clothing from him without leaving a single scratch.

He looked back up at her in horror. "You devil!" he shouted, backing up while scooping the remains of his clothes from the ground. He held them to his chest, then turned and ran, wild-eyed, from her.

"You should thank me for leaving your breeches alone!" she called after him.

A soft laugh came over her shoulder. Portia turned to see an elderly man lounging on a stoop, leaning against the entryway. He had white hair down to his shoulders, worn but clean clothes, and a twinkling smile he beamed at her.

"Nice work. That kid always irritated me. But I have to say, you're the first one I've seen that has taken care of him right off."

Portia smiled back at him. "Thanks." The man waved her over. He made room for her on the stoop. Portia hesitated for a split second then sat down, joining him in watching the passersby by on the street.

"New here, aren't you?" he asked.

"That obvious?" That concerned Portia a little. She didn't want to be a target for the locals.

The man glanced at her, seeing her look. "Only because I've been here forever. Most of these young people don't pay that much attention. You're a breath of fresh air though. You remind me of my daughter."

Daughter. Portia had never been anyone's daughter, not that she could remember. A lump swelled in her throat. She fought it back, blinking rapidly while facing away from the old man. She didn't have the luxury of emotions right now. "Oh, how so?" she asked, working to keep her voice steady.

"For starters, she didn't like that boy much either," the old man said with a laugh. This made Portia smile. She thought she would have liked his daughter. "Also, she was good with a knife—though she probably spent too much of her time with one cooking. I miss her cooking."

Portia sighed. Anything cooked right now sounded good. Her stomach agreed and answered with a rumble. The old man looked down at her belly then up at her eyes with raised eyebrows. "Another fan of cooking, are we?" he asked.

Portia laughed, then nodded, tears and laughter mixing on her face. After the seriousness of the last few days, it felt good to laugh.

"That's the good thing about the young—always up for some eating. Speaking of which, I have extra stew on the stove. Come in and have some," the old man said. He stuck out his hand towards her for a shake. "Elyas Penry."

Portia shook his hand. "Portia Harris." She regretted telling him her real name immediately, but it was too late to do anything about it now.

"Nice to meet you, Portia. Come in and share a bite with an old man." He stood, opened the door, and motioned for her to enter. She could see inside the dwelling. It was clean, neat, welcoming. A red enamel pot hung over the fire. The smell of herbs and stewed meat overwhelmed her. Portia hesitated.

Elyas considered her, then gave a little chuckle. "I've seen what you can do with your knife. I have no death wish, so believe me when I tell you I'm not inviting you in with any ill intent. I'm a simple old man without any tricks up his sleeve."

Portia nodded at that. He was only asking her to share a meal. She had her dagger if she needed it. She also had her magic. Her stomach, growling in complaint, reinforced the notion that going in was a good idea. But Portia still hesitated.

"I have little to share in return," she said, reluctant to become indebted to a stranger.

Elyas made a small clicking noise with his mouth, waved her in more emphatically. "No worries. What I want more than anything is a bit of conversation. Pay for your dinner with that."

Portia nodded. She stood before the doorway then looked up at Elyas. "Why is your daughter no longer here?" she asked.

A dark look crossed his face, then he banished it with a small smile. "The plague."

8

"The plague?" Portia asked, as she entered Elyas's home. "Yes. The healers were slow on that one. It spread through the city. Sad too, more sad than normal, since it seemed to hit the youngest the hardest. My daughter thought she was safe since she rarely went out. But no one is safe with the plague." He shook his head. "But let's talk of happier things, like dinner."

Portia sat at the wooden table in the kitchen. Elyas handed her a yellow stoneware bowl full to the rim with the brown stew, then sat down with his own bowl. She could see carrots and potatoes and chunks of meat—her mouth watered immediately. He nodded at her to start, and she did so, shoveling in a huge spoonful. It was spiced perfectly. She practically hummed in happiness.

They ate in silence. Without even asking, Elyas topped off Portia's bowl before it was empty. She merely nodded and kept eating. Finally, when they were both sated, they leaned back in their chairs in contentment. Portia rubbed her full belly. It had been a long time since she had been able to eat as much as she wanted. In Valencia, there never seemed to be money for enough food. And while the tavern food had been good, it had not been nearly enough—filling up on ale was not the same thing as gorging on real food.

"So, what are your plans in this city, young lass?" Elyas asked. He picked his teeth with the tines of his fork, trying to get the last bits of meat out.

"I need a job, I guess," Portia answered. She thought about the six months she needed to bide until the Academy gave the magic test again. She would need enough money for a roof over her head and food to eat. She was down to her last copper.

"Job? What skills do you have? Cook? Tailor? Serving wench? Although, I don't think you have the temperament for that one. Drunkards like to keep their clothes about them," Elyas said, giving a little chuckle at the memory of Portia's knife work.

Portia looked up at Elyas through half-lidded eyes. The warmth in the fire relaxed her from the outside while the warmth in her belly relaxed her from inside. His twinkling eyes were kind and welcoming. He seemed trustworthy. She thought he might be levelheaded enough to not react ill to her past. Her neck tingled, as if to confirm her hunch she could trust him. "I have thieving skills. Good ones." She checked for his reaction at those words. He only smiled knowingly.

"Is that how you learned the knife skills? That's a dangerous profession, so it's good you can take care of yourself." He gave her a teasing look. "I hope you're not here to rob me of more than dinner."

"Hey!" Portia said, feeling slightly indignant. "You offered dinner for conversation, so let's talk. But that does not include insulting your guest."

"No insult intended, lass. Just some good old-fashioned teasing," Elyas said, gathering up the dinner bowls and placing them in the sink. He turned to face her again, leaning against the counter. "If you want work like that, it can be had here, without having to sell what you get on the black market." He turned back towards the sink again, pouring water on the bowls. "It's what I used to do when things got too tight. You do what you must to survive in this world."

Portia relaxed at those words. Far from being judged, she had found someone who understood where she was coming from.

"Go to the house with the sign of a mouse and a hen on it. It will get you what you need. Tell them I sent you," Elyas said, bringing two glasses of mead to the table and sitting down. "If you've got no money yet, you can stay here until you are on your feet. I'm a lonely old man who'd appreciate the company. And if you're feeling guilty, you can always cook."

Portia laughed at that. He did not want her cooking. Even Mark had complained when she had attempted it in the Black Cats' kitchen and asked why she did not get food from Cook instead. "I'll think about it. I should probably go before it gets dark."

"I'd say it's too late for that," Elyas said, nodding towards the window where the sky was turning a dark blue over the curtains blocking the bottom half of the glass pane. "Stay tonight, then find your job in the morning."

Portia agreed to stay the night after he showed her the bedroom with the locking door and the fluffy goose down mattress. She lay down with her dagger lying on her chest, firmly gripped in her right hand. She didn't think she had anything to fear, but it was always best to be prepared. She nodded off within seconds of closing her eyes.

The sun beamed down on Coverack in the morning. There was not a cloud in the bright blue sky. Portia made her way through the Warrens, her belly full of the cold meat pie that Elyas had fed her that morning. Children ran through the streets, some without shoes or much clothing at all, while their mothers carried baskets of laundry they had taken in. Shops were everywhere. Some looked like they were doing a decent business, while others were boarded over and abandoned. Nothing looked new.

She searched for the sign of the mouse and the hen. All the signs she saw were of an animal of some sort, or else the moon and stars or some other symbol. She didn't understand how anyone knew where anything was. A young girl gave Portia a small smile as she passed by with a basket of mead bottles. Portia ran after her. "Miss, would you happen to know where the sign of a mouse and a hen is. I don't understand the signs here. I mean, how do you know which shop the butcher is, or anything else?"

The girl stopped, eyed Portia. "No one can afford new signs all the time. Businesses come and go—they use what was there before. We know what's where."

"Do you know the mouse and the hen?" Portia asked.

The girl nodded, pointed off in the direction towards the Academy, then went on her way.

Portia set off in the direction pointed out by the girl. Three streets down, she found the right shop. The sign overhead with the mouse and the hen was the best-looking part of the entire storefront. The door needed a coat of paint, its existing paint peeling in long strips. The windows were dirty, making the inside appear dim and unclean. Portia took a deep breath then entered.

The inside was indeed no better than the outside. Piles of linen topped every surface, most of it old. A few newer pieces by the door were still bright with sun bleaching but showed holes and irregularities where stitching had been pulled out. She knew the linen was stolen by the existence of the holes— they showed where the insignias from their house of origin had been poorly removed. Portia snorted at the bad workmanship.

Her snort alerted the shopkeeper in the back. He passed into the main shop through a curtain leading to the backroom. He was a skinny man who looked half-starved. He looked Portia up and down, sizing her up as a possible customer. Portia gave him a smile that she hoped was reassuring.

"Morning," Portia greeted the shopkeeper. "I was looking for a job and thought you might need help."

The shopkeeper's expectant expression turned to disdain. "Job. Ah, no. We don't need help here." He motioned for her to leave before turning to return to the back.

"I have talents you could use here. I know that just from

walking in the door," Portia said, mustering a challenge in her voice.

The shopkeeper slowly turned back towards her. "And how do you make that out?" he asked.

"I can remove stitching so well, you can't even tell it had ever been there," Portia said. The shopkeeper shrugged his shoulders, unimpressed. She pressed on. "I can even get product." She gave him her best confident look.

His face relaxed into a smile. "That's a lot of promises. How about some proof?" He waved to the back of the shop, indicating Portia to enter. She nodded and preceded him to the rear.

Three girls sat at small benches in the tiny room, working under dirty windows. They were pulling out stitches from stolen linen. The shopkeeper tossed Portia a hand towel from a pile near one of the girls. Portia grabbed a small knife from the workbench and quickly plucked all the stitches from the house insignia on the hand towel. She pulled the loose threads through and gave the towel a final rub with her thumb, feeling the tingle at the back of her neck as she mentally nudged the threads of the towel to go back into place, the way they had been before any embroidery had been done there. It looked perfect. She handed the towel to the shopkeeper. He eyed it appreciatively, giving her a nod of approval.

"How much of a cut do you want?" he asked, getting right to the heart of the matter. "If your procuring skills be as good as your stitching skills, that is."

"Where I came from, good linen went for a silver a piece. Give me a copper for each one I bring in," Portia said. That was higher than she had gotten in Valencia, but she was going to at least ask for that much.

The shopkeeper considered, rubbing the linen where Portia had removed the stitching. He sighed. "How'd ya find me?" he asked finally.

"Elyas sent me," Portia said. "Elyas Penry."

The shopkeeper nodded then tossed the linen towel back onto the pile on the workbench with a grunt. "Good enough. Come back tomorrow—with goods."

The following weeks passed quickly for Portia. She felt comfortable enough with Elyas that soon she forgot all about her plans to find another place to live. They got into a comfortable routine. She would leave in the morning to either go thieve linens or remove stitches in the shop, and return in the evening to a home-cooked meal. Elyas never asked where she had been that day, and when she left coppers on the table for food, he only nodded and dropped them in a jar on a shelf in the kitchen. He always had mead for after their meal. Then he would ask her for a story from Valencia or share one of his own. Portia favored Elyas's stories that involved his daughter. His daughter had been a wild one—running through the Warrens and terrorizing the bullies. At least that's how Elyas told her it had been. She wondered how much was exaggeration, grown large through retelling after retelling in the distance of time.

But that was back when the Warrens had not been as rough as they were now. Their present state directly resulted from the ill will of one of the houses of Coverack. Elyas's voice turned bitter when he told her of what they had done.

Coverack had four great houses: Riddlepit, Ladock, Kelynack, and Hayle. The royal house was simply known as the Royal House of Coverack. Riddlepit had always considered the House of Ladock, to whom Elyas served, as its main competitor in gaining favor from the Royal House of Coverack.

As a liege to Ladock, Elyas lived in one of its districts, the Warrens. It was where many of the Ladock citizens and servants lived. To undercut the House of Ladock, Riddlepit had done all they could to destroy the Warrens. They had strangled access to the district where they could. It was easy for them since the Riddlepit districts abutted the Warrens. They could use that to control access to the streets of the Warrens. This made it difficult for customers to reach shops and difficult for shops to bring in goods. It also brought down the morale of the residents of the Warrens. Riddlepit had further sent undesirables to live in the Warrens, paying their initial rents and getting them established before abandoning them to become a drain on the resources of their new neighborhood. Riddlepit had even gone so far as to magically harass people who lived there, disturbing their sleep and affecting their health. This was too much to bear for many of the retainers of House Ladock. Despite their loyalty, many of those in service had fled. The leadership of Ladock had made a grave mistake in not defending their people vigorously enough. The Ladock house was now in great disarray as the younger members fought for control, desiring to fix the errors of the past.

"Why didn't you move when it became so bad?" Portia

asked as she dipped her bread into the last of the soup in front of her.

Elyas sighed, pushing his empty bowl away. "I had wanted to, especially for my daughter's sake. But by the time it was clear we had to move houses, Ladock had released me from service. And then we could no longer afford it. It was a sad time for us. That is when I learned about the world of thieving. I did it so my daughter wouldn't have to." He got up, put his bowl on the sink, and grabbed the bottle of mead and two glasses. Returning to the table, he poured them each a drink. "At least I could support us."

"Release you from service? How could they do that after you had stayed despite all that was going on in the Warrens?" Portia asked, not understanding. How could a lifetime of loyalty be betrayed like that?

"Politics. You have to be good at the game to survive in this city," Elyas said, taking a deep drink of his mead. "I was the personal servant of one of the senior members of the house. When he died, the younger house members saw me as a threat. They wanted reform. And I was old. I guess I am old."

Fear trilled in Portia's heart. The fact of Elyas's age scared her, only because she knew with age came death. She was not ready to lose him. She was not ready to lose a comfortable place now that she had just found it. "You're not old," she said emphatically.

Elyas laughed. "Thank you for saying that, lass, but your words do not make it so. It's okay getting old. Many are not lucky enough to have that experience." He looked down at his glass glumly.

Portia nodded, pretending agreement, although she wasn't sure she agreed.

That night, as she lay in bed, she decided she would pay back the House of Riddlepit for the pain they had caused Elyas. She nodded off dreaming of revenge. Her plan was not forgotten when she awoke.

In her thieving runs, she had not ventured outside of the Warrens. But she had learned enough to find the districts of the other great houses of Coverack. She entered the district just to the north, a district of the House Riddlepit, where she knew there were many homes of their elite. She picked one that looked like a castle—its owner's arrogance clear in its styling with turrets, a vast entryway, and even a fake moat. She could feel the anger welling in her throat just looking at it. The people in this house thought they were special. She thought they especially deserved revenge visited upon them.

Jumping over the useless dirt moat, she scaled the wall thick with ivy. Portia thought any house manager worth his salt would have had that ivy removed long ago. It was too easy for thieves to climb it. It was as if they were asking to be robbed.

She climbed into a second-story window. It was a bedroom, awash with velvet curtains, thick wool rugs, and a bed piled high with fine linen coverings. Portia stepped towards the bed, half in awe and half in anger that any single person could have such a nice room. There were many who slept in the streets in the city, and yet here was enough linen for ten people. All for a single person.

Portia swallowed. She had to complete her task and get out of here. She grabbed her leather bag, the one she had purchased just for this run since it was larger, more spacious, and sturdier. She yanked it open and walked to the bed, then grabbed the linen closest to her and shoved it into her bag. It was bulkier than she expected. Portia wished she had brought a rope to tie it up in a bundle. A loud coughing noise from behind her caught her attention. She froze then slowly turned to face a girl her age in a long blue silk dress and with a face red with rage.

"Explain yourself," the girl demanded. Her fists clenched at her side, white-knuckled.

Portia bluffed. The girl was slight, smaller than her. If she could buy time and escape out the window, she would be fine. The girl was too small to physically stop her. Portia just needed her to be quiet long enough for her to get away.

"What would you like to hear?" Portia asked, trying to affect a solicitous tone.

"Don't be smart with me," the young girl spit out. "You're a thief. You will pay for this."

"I am not," Portia said, edging towards the window. "How would you know I was a thief anyhow? Perhaps I'm here to do the laundry. Who are you?"

"I am Magisend Lucy Gwynn of House Riddlepit. Those are my bedsheets you are defiling."

Portia laughed. She couldn't help it. That was the most

ridiculous name she had ever heard. The girl's eyes widened even more at Portia's mirth; her faced turned purple in rage.

"You will pay for laughing, and for stealing, you worthless girl," Magisend said as she walked towards Portia.

Portia made a dash towards the open window. Magisend lifted her arms and then motioned in front of Portia's feet. A stream of ice shot out from her fingertips. Portia jumped, leaving the ice to pool where her feet had been. That was magic she'd never seen before. Perhaps she had misjudged this situation.

Portia used Mark's magic to create bright dots all over her face to blind the irate girl.

Rather than react with howls of pain as others had, the girl only laughed. "You sorely lack talent—and judgment—if you think that is enough to stop someone like me." Magisend waved her right arm at the window, sending another blast of ice that filled the opening, cutting off Portia's escape route.

Portia turned and ran for the door to the room. Magisend cut her off with another pillar of ice. Portia's heart beat quickly, and she willed herself to not panic. She jumped back from the now blocked door and veered right. She nearly ran into a third pillar of ice that Magisend created. Portia had a hard time breathing; the air in the room was turning cold from all the ice. Her lungs hurt with each inhale. She ran in still a different direction, and this time did not stop herself in time from careening into a gigantic pillar of ice. Blood ran down her cheek from the collision. She slipped and fell in shock, landing on her left side, pain radiating along her entire body.

Desperate, Portia poured her magic—every ounce of

strength she had—into Mark's bright lights. The lights were so warm she could feel her skin sizzle. She concentrated on creating them on her hands. Crawling to her feet, she half-ran, half-slid, to the window. She pushed her hands against the ice block in the window. The ice melted in rivers of water that flooded the room. Blessedly, it also cooled her hands.

Magisend inhaled sharply. "No!"

Portia knew what was coming. She took one hand from the ice block and thrust it behind her, blocking the stream of ice coming from Magisend. She gritted her teeth, trying to not black out, as her energy streamed from her fingertips in each direction. She concentrated on the hole in the ice, willing it to grow larger, faster, before she passed out. Suddenly, the ice surface cracked in hundreds of hairline fractures. Portia could feel it give slightly under her hand. She braced herself, then gave one last magical push towards Magisend before physically pushing at the ice in the window frame. The surface shattered. The window opening was clear. Portia released her magic and jumped headfirst out the window.

She landed with a roll on the ground below the window, grateful she had practiced such maneuvers before. Without that experience, she would have broken her neck. She felt pain on her tailbone and along her spine and right arm, now matching the pain she had in her left arm. She didn't linger to see exactly where she was hurt though. She scrambled to her feet and limped away.

Above her, Magisend screamed for the guards.

Portia hurried down the street, gasping with pain from each step. When she had gotten several blocks away, she noticed the people on the street giving her queer looks. Looking down, she saw that she was bleeding profusely from her hand. Blood stained her clothing. Worst of all, she was dripping a trail of droplets behind her. She hissed in dismay. Grabbing a corner from one linen in her bag, she tore a long strip off and bandaged her hand. She also dabbed at the blood on her face. It had run down her neck and into her shirt. Stopping briefly in front of a storefront window pane to see her reflection, she cleaned herself off as best she could. At the very least, she needed to stop dripping blood.

She concentrated on healing her hand, but she was too exhausted from the battle to do so. Her magic flickered weakly. Even so, she was able to muster enough to stop the immediate bleeding.

Portia caught people staring at her in the window's reflection. She had to hurry. Looking cleaner, she left the window and walked down the street, trying to be casual while still listening intently for the sounds of pursuit behind her. But none came. She wondered why the guards of Riddlepit had not found her yet. She considered going off in the wrong direction, to mislead them on the whereabouts of her home just in case they were truly in pursuit, but she was too exhausted for that. She was hurt and needed to get rid of the stolen goods and get out of sight.

Portia pushed open the door to the linen shop and staggered in. The shopkeeper looked up at her in surprise. He gasped as he came closer to look at her injuries. Seeing the bloodstained clothes and her bandages, he looked out the front to see if anyone was coming. There was no one. He then quickly ushered Portia into the back room, swiftly drawing the curtain that separated the two spaces.

"What happened to you?" he asked with concern.

Portia leaned against one workbench, not wanting to bend her knees enough to sit in a chair. "Riddlepit. Some stupid girl in one of their houses... that's what happened."

The shopkeeper recoiled. "And you're here to talk about it? Do you know how lucky you are?"

Portia did not expect that reaction. How bloodthirsty was this house? What had she done by openly stealing from them? "They are that bad?"

"It looks like you got a taste of their methods. A small taste."

Portia was regretting her decision to wreak revenge on Riddlepit. She could see fear on the faces of the girls in the back when she had mentioned the house. It was one thing to steal linen from a house that could easily afford to lose it—it was another to put herself or Elyas, or even the shopkeeper and his staff, in physical danger.

"Anyone follow you here?" the shopkeeper asked, wringing his hands in anxiety.

"No. I am not that dumb. I would not lead them here." Portia hoped that was true and not just wishful thinking. Her flight from the Riddlepit house was a blur in her mind now. "I should go anyway."

The shopkeeper's face battled between concern and greed. Greed finally won. "Will you be able to work this week?"

Portia grunted. She opened her bag in response to his

question, dumping out its contents on the table. The lush linens looked even more resplendent in contrast to the dingy interior of the back room. One girl removing stitches inhaled with a gasp.

The shopkeeper waved her to be quiet in irritation, but he himself came closer to look at the unusual haul. "Amazing. I've not seen this quality before—if ever."

Portia nodded. Her head throbbed with the movement.

The shopkeeper found a piece with a house insignia on it. He gave a whistle of approval. "You have done well for yourself, girl, very well. This quality will fetch a fine price. I'll pay you extra for these and for any others of the like you can get."

"What about the danger from the house?" Portia asked, surprised at the shopkeeper's sudden bravery in keeping the stolen linen from the dangerous house.

"I'll sell them quickly, don't you worry," he said, distracted. Portia imagined him already counting the profits in his head. She smiled at that, even though it hurt her face.

She grinned even more when the shopkeeper dropped two pieces of silver in her hand. She gripped them tightly.

E lyas put down a steaming mug of mead in front of Portia. "Drink this up," he told her. "You'll need it." He said the last part low, under his breath, as he looked at her bandaged hand. Portia gingerly took the mug with her left hand and brought it to her lips, blowing to cool the hot drink.

He turned back to the fire and hung a large kettle on the hook over the flames. He filled it with water. "We'll let that boil, then we can take care of your injuries."

Portia had said nothing when she had limped in the front door. Elyas had taken one look at her and brought her into the kitchen. He made her sit and then ladled a plate full of food and set it down in front of her. He motioned for her to eat, watching her consume every bite.

Once dinner was over and the dirty dishes were pushed in a pile in the sink, Elyas sat opposite her at the table, nursing his own drink. He gave a sigh. "Okay, what happened?"

"I was working," Portia said, not sure how much she

wanted to share. "Someone didn't like how I was doing things."

"You got that at the shop?" Elyas asked, indignant.

"No... no. I was thieving."

Elyas squinted his eyes in disappointment, shaking his head. "Okay, I was hoping you weren't. I knew there was other work at the shop. That's why I had sent you to that place."

Portia felt a sharp pain in her stomach at the thought she had disappointed Elyas. She knew it was childish, but she couldn't help protesting. "There was not much work, at least none that paid any real money. It's much easier to make money—or at least it's a lot faster—from thieving than from sewing."

"I know, lass. But I hate to see you take the risk." He nodded at her injuries. "And look what happened."

"It's the first time I've been hurt. I've been doing this for months, and no one's ever caught me, much less injured me." Portia said.

She could take care of herself. She didn't want to look weak in front of Elyas. She already felt like a burden. He had never said she was, but she was not used to so much kindness. It felt uncomfortable sometimes.

"So, what was different this time?" he asked as he got up to check the water over the fire.

"I went into... I chose... I stole from a Riddlepit house."

Elyas pivoted to her. "You what? No, don't do that." He stared at her intently. "That house is too dangerous. You leave any of the households that belong to that group alone. Nothing good comes from them."

Portia chuckled under her breath. "They had some nice linens. That came from them at least."

"You invaded their territory to steal linens? Oh, lass, that is bold. But promise me you won't do it again."

Portia nodded her promise. He wouldn't have to ask twice. She had realized when coming home that Magisend could have easily killed her. The only reason she was still alive was that Magisend had held back—and that she herself had some natural talent for magic—and a bit of luck. But she had nowhere the control nor the strength of magic that Magisend had. She didn't even think the tiny girl had broken a sweat, while she had been putting all of her own energy into just surviving. If Magisend was that powerful, she hated to think how skilled the older members of that household were. Especially if they had gone to the Magic Academy. It was a sharp lesson on how much she had to learn.

"What exactly happened?"

Portia sighed. "A girl with an incredibly long name nearly killed me with ice. Magic ice. I didn't even know you could do things like that."

"Ay, she probably goes to that school of magic. They learn all kinds of tricks," Elyas said, dipping a towel into the hot water over the stove then bringing it over to Portia and motioning for her to give him her injured hand. She held it out tentatively. It throbbed in pain. She doubted the hot, wet rag would feel much better. "How did you get away?" Elyas asked as he gingerly unwrapped the blood-encrusted linen from around her hand.

Portia winced, sucking in her breath, as Elyas worked. "I have some magic too," Portia said.

Elyas looked at her face, raising his eyebrows at that. "Oh?"

Portia's face turned red. Why did she feel like she had done something wrong by not telling him sooner?

"What sort of magic?" he asked, once again turning his attention to her hand.

"Lights. I don't know what they call that. Some things with plants and fibers too." She shrugged. Somehow, she didn't have the words to describe what she could do. When he looked up at her, she formed a light mote on one of her cheeks to show him.

"I see. How did you learn to do that?" he asked.

"I don't know. I watch others."

He nodded. "So, you've never trained with anybody?"

Portia shook her head.

"This is deep. You're lucky you can still use your hand," Elyas said, looking up at Portia. "It'll take a while to heal." Elyas poured some liquid over her wounded hand from a small jar he had placed on the table earlier. It burned like crazy. Portia gasped then bit her lip to keep from crying out. "Sorry, lass, it has to be done."

Elyas finished cleaning the wound and re-bandaging it. Portia had drunk the rest of her mead while she watched. Her head bobbed in exhaustion as the adrenaline wore off. Elyas carried her to her bedroom, laying her on top of the bed with all her clothes on, and left the room, gently shutting the door. Portia was asleep as soon as her eyes closed.

The next weeks passed in a blur. Portia tried healing her hand at night, using her magic, but it wasn't enough on its own. The deep hand wound was trickier business than healing bruises. So Elyas had Portia exercising her hand as the wound healed the old-fashioned way. The exercises were necessary to keep the scar tissue from shrinking up, which would have reduced the use of her hand for the rest of her life. He had her stretching it, kneading dough and other household chores that pushed the use of her hand, even doing weights with her fingers.

He also had her practice her magic. Under his direction, she worked on it daily to strengthen her skills and to build up her endurance. He insisted that she push her abilities to their limits. He had told her most limits in life, as in magic, were not real, but rather were the brain's way of being lazy. It was easier to say it was not possible than to suffer the discomfort of exercising a new skill. He told her she did not have to settle for that. When she had shown him the light motes she had learned from Mark, she had only created them on her own skin or between her and whoever she was using them against. She had not realized the distance she could place them. He had her practice by moving a light mote towards him, gradually getting farther and farther away. Eventually, she could create them on demand and surround him with them while he sat in the next room over. She didn't even have to see inside the room itself. Portia didn't understand how the light motes knew exactly where to go, how to not manifest inside a chair, or a table, or a person. But somehow, they did. They never went where they should not be.

The more she practiced, the more confident she became in her abilities.

She also learned the difference between a magic pool and magic abilities. Apparently, her magic pool was not that strong. That was why it took so much of her energy to do magic. There were others, she learned, that could do the same magic, but it took much less effort from them. To some, it was the equivalent to blinking. It was not welcome news to learn that others could innately be so much more powerful. But it motivated her to practice even more. If her magic was not strong, then it was even more important that she be skilled and accurate.

Magic abilities referred to the types of magic she could do. She said nothing to Elyas about a Jack of Magic. And he did not think it was unusual she could work with light and create duplicates like Peter. His understanding of magic had been limited to what his daughter, Chenna, had taught him. His daughter had the ability to work with fire, which made for an exciting household before she had learned to control her childhood impulses. When Chenna was older, she had liked to show off in the kitchen with it while cooking. Elyas would not tell Portia why his daughter had not gone to the Academy. But still, she had picked up enough knowledge just from being in the same city as the Academy to improve herself. And she had shared her knowledge with her father. Portia was grateful to his daughter for the knowledge she was now getting.

No matter how Portia struggled with any skill she worked on, Elyas was always encouraging. He also would not tolerate when she said she couldn't do it. He always said she could, perhaps not that day, but that she could—and would—do it, eventually. She took this to heart.

Portia wanted to go back to work at the shop, but Elyas wouldn't let her at first. "If they know the thief's hand was injured, then you can't go anywhere until it is completely healed. You might have gotten away, or they might be biding their time, or they might be out looking for you," he said to her one evening as she was kneading a loaf of bread, stretching her palms out with each down push, feeling the scar pull in protest. "Once your wounds are healed, you'll have a much better chance of blending into the crowd."

"Do you really think they would care that much about a lowly linen thief?" Portia asked.

"You don't understand. That house is so feared that no one in the city would have dreamt of doing what you had done. It's more the insult than the injury that will infuriate them. I know that girl did a lot of harm to you, but believe me, she was being kind. At least kind by their standards." Elyas said, drinking a glass of mead, his feet stretched out before him. He enjoyed having someone else cook.

"I hope to never meet the rest," Portia said as she shoved the dough into a large bowl to rise, covering it with linen.

"I hope that for you as well."

"Did you find your mended tunic?" Portia asked. She sat down across from Elyas. The sun was just setting, leaving the windows to darken into blue and then black as night fell. The smell of warm yeast filled the kitchen, along with the smell of the potato and meat soup that would be their dinner.

"I did, lass, and you're not to do mending for me while that hand is still healing. I can take care of my clothes myself." Elyas gave her a wink. She appreciated his fierce independence. They were alike in that way. They worked together as a team, each one contributing and no one feeling like a burden. She couldn't remember the last time she had been this happy. It felt like home—a word she would not use out loud, and barely dared whisper in her own mind. But that was what it was to her.

Soon she would go back to the shop to earn more coins. Her hand was healed, nearly fully so, and the herbs that Elyas had pressed into the wound, along with rich oils, had discouraged scarring. Someone would have to look closely at her hand to find any evidence of her injury. She was determined to not give anyone that chance.

The only dark spot in her life was the recurring nightmares. She had woken Elyas more than once with her thrashing and moaning in her sleep. Even in the next room over, he could hear her distress. He had comforted her as best he could, but they puzzled him as much as they puzzled her. Neither one of them could imagine the meaning of a crack in the sky and the velvet darkness behind it. She thought maybe it had to do with guilt for leaving Mark.

She had shared her fears with Elyas about leaving Mark and her thought of going back and retrieving him. Elyas worried at this plan, but Portia knew she should do so, and sooner rather than later. He had made her promise she wouldn't go back until she had enough for a carriage ride to Valencia. Elyas even offered to go with her, but Portia didn't want him to have to endure the trip. Besides, it would mean having to save twice as much money. She dreaded to think what had become of Mark without her protection against Deyelna. But her heart beat in fear at the thought of going back. And then she felt ashamed for being a coward.

Portia resumed working at the shop. The shopkeeper was disappointed when she didn't bring in another batch of Riddlepit linen, but he never pressed her to do so. His business had picked up in her absence, and he was more than grateful for any products that she could get to restock the shelves. She knew some customers came back repeatedly, hoping to get more of the exceedingly fine linen she had obtained from Magisend Lucy's bedroom, but she steeled herself against the guilt of not doing it again. She dare not risk it. It helped that the shopkeeper never asked.

One day she had an especially good haul from a woman who had been rude to her in the marketplace a few months earlier. Some days she felt guilty about taking from other citizens, but not today. She had even stopped off at a bakery and purchased Elyas's favorite nut pastry as a treat for them to celebrate her successful day. When she got home, she laid the wrapped paper from the bakery on the table in the kitchen. Elyas was at the fire, stirring that night's dinner.

"I have a surprise for you," she said, grinning from ear to ear. Watching Elyas's outsized delight in all bakery products was one of her favorite things. She wished any food item made her that happy.

He turned to look at her, quickly seeing the wrapped treat on the table. His eyes lit up as she had expected, giving her a warm glow in her heart for making him happy. "Wonderful! You treat me too well, lass," he said, as he hurried to the table and opened the package to see its contents. "We shall have a wonderful dessert tonight, thanks to you."

"You're sharing?" Portia said with a tease in her voice.

"Of course I'm sharing! When don't I share?" he asked, his hand over his heart with an expression of fake hurt.

Portia didn't bother to answer. She knew his game. It made her smile anyway.

"I have something for you as well," he said, pushing a folded parchment towards her on the kitchen table.

She looked at it in surprise. "What's that?"

"Open it and find out."

She took the parchment. It had a red official stamp on it, with fancy curling script she could not read. Opening the letter, she recognized the blue buildings on the engraved letterhead. It was from the Magic Academy. It had her name on it. She could not read the rest of the fancy writing since only her name was written in print block letters. She was embarrassed that she didn't understand what it said. Heat rose from her cheeks.

Elyas saw her blushing, and grinned, not understanding the reason for her embarrassment. "Overwhelmed you, didn't I?" he asked.

"Yes," Portia said, trying to recover. "This is..."

"Your invitation to try out for the Academy. I got you on the rolls when you were out working. Your magic ability has come so far, I think you have a real chance to get in." Elyas put down bowls on the table for dinner. "The trials start in two days."

Portia's embarrassment turned to elation. And surprise. Somehow, she had been living here for six months. Six months!

And then, just as quickly, her elation turned to unease. She was comfortable here. Did she really want to go to the Magic Academy? But she saw the excited look on Elyas's face and knew she couldn't disappoint him. She gave him her best smile, willing her heart to be happy. She went to him and hugged him. "Thank you, thank you. I had forgotten all about it."

He hugged her back then released her quickly. She thought she saw his eyes water as he turned to the fire to grab a ladle for their dinner. She realized she was not the only one who had mixed feelings. It made her appreciate him even more. He would do what was best for her, no matter what the cost to him personally.

"You need some new clothes. I want you walking on that field looking like you're already a member of the Academy," he said, pulling the jar of coins off the shelf. He poured out a handful of silver and copper. She realized that he had not spent any of the money she had given him. "You have time to get some new clothes tomorrow, some nice ones."

"No. I can't take this. This was for you, and for food and for the house," Portia said, protesting the coins Elyas was trying to push into her hands.

"I can take care of myself. I thought of it as just keeping

the money for you, for when you needed it. You need it now. You must look good when you go to the Magic Academy, like you belong. It'll keep your confidence strong. There would be plenty of those from the five houses who will try to intimidate you because you are not rich like they are—or at least try." Elyas winked at Portia. "I'd say being poor is not a good reason to fail the tests," Elyas said, placing the silver on the table in front of where Portia normally sat when she refused to open her hand for him. "But first we celebrate—sit," he gestured to her seat, "it's time to eat."

The next day, Portia went to the clothier that Elyas had recommended. It was outside of the Warrens, but he said it was worth the trip because that was the clothier that most Academy applicants went to for their trial apparel. It was a tradition for the children of the five great houses of the city. He wanted nothing less for Portia, so she agreed to go.

When she got to the shop, it was the largest she had ever seen. It looked like it took up most of the block it was on. Portia's neck tingled as she got closer to its doors, but she couldn't place why immediately. Then she saw them—several men dressed in all black. They were across the street, seated at the outdoor tables of a tavern. Their waiter, a thin young man, dropped off their drinks and walked off as quickly as he could. The men looked menacing. And they were staring at the people entering the clothier shop. Portia swallowed. She did not want to be the subject of their attention. They reminded her too much of the man in black from Valencia.

She pulled up the hood of her jacket then joined a group of parents and children walking into the shop, keeping the parents between her and the watching men. A few of the parents gave her irritated looks at her proximity, but Portia ignored the glares and pushed her way to the front to enter first.

Inside, parents and children filled the shop, keeping the numerous clerks busy and squabbling over colors and styles. The parents had strong ideas about what their children should wear based on what they had worn for their own trials when they themselves were children.

Portia felt out of place being there by herself. She wondered if she should have brought Elyas and then shook herself. No, he had encouraged her to be independent. She could do this. And if she couldn't even buy clothing, how would she survive at the Academy on her own?

"Can I help you?" a young clerk asked her, giving her a gentle smile. "Are your parents picking out something for you?" The clerk looked around for anyone that might be with Portia.

"No. I mean yes, but I'm here alone," Portia said. "I would like help though, please."

"Alone?" the clerk said, looking surprised and hesitant. "I'm not sure—"

Portia held out her hand filled with silver. The clerk came closer to peer at the silver then changed her attitude to one of extreme helpfulness. "I see. Well, of course I would love to help you. Let me show you all the finest items we have, including the new styles just this year for the trials," the clerk said, putting her arm in Portia's arm and drawing her deeper into the shop.

The selection was overwhelming. But Portia found a beautiful outfit, in the newest style, constructed in her favorite colors of red and black. She almost didn't recognize herself in the mirror after trying them on. The months of eating well with Elyas, along with finally getting enough sleep in the safety of their home, had changed her markedly. The black circles under her eyes were gone. Her skin was no longer pale but rather flush with color. Her eyes were bright. She did not look like the girl who had lived with the Black Cats. Now, she looked just like all the other children in the shop—healthy. Her eyes watered with happiness.

She gladly paid the silver the clerk asked for, happy that there were still some coins left in her hand when she was done. She packed her old clothes in her leather bag. The clothier was an hour's journey from home, and she wanted to get back before dark.

Checking outside, she saw that the men across the street were gone. It was getting late, so perhaps they had simply finished their meal. Or they had grown bored of glaring at those preparing for the Academy tryouts. In any case, Portia was simply glad. She did not want to deal with a chase—not on such a happy day.

She exited the shop. Looking around, it did indeed look like the men were gone. Citizens on the street were rushing along to go home for the evening. Portia joined the crowd.

Portia had just entered the Warrens again when she saw a little girl crying in the street. She couldn't have been over two or three. Tears ran down her face and onto her dress. Her clothing was old but clean and patched. This little girl was well cared for except for the lack of a guardian at the moment. Portia looked around but couldn't see anyone. Everyone else in the street was ignoring the little girl. Portia walked closer to talk to her.

"What's wrong?" Portia asked as she crouched low to get to the little girl's eye level. The little girl was crying so hard she was shaking and hiccupping. Portia gave her a gentle squeeze on both shoulders to calm her. "What's wrong? Where're your parents?"

"Mama," was all the little girl could get out between hiccups.

Portia sighed then stood while holding the little girl's hand. Portia kept her close as she looked around again for a parent. Portia checked the sun. It was still at least an hour from setting, high enough in the horizon that she felt it was okay to try to find this girl's home. She had time. And the oncoming darkness was even more reason for her to help the little girl.

They walked together hand-in-hand down the street. The little girl's crying gradually subsided until she was only hiccuping occasionally. Portia looked down at her. "Do you see your mother anywhere?" The little girl looked all around herself then shook her head no. They continued this routine for several blocks, prompting Portia to wonder if they should circle back and try a different direction.

When they reached the end of that block, and there was still no sign of the child's mother, Portia decided they should head back to the starting spot in case the mother was there waiting for them. To her disappointment, there was no one where she had originally found the girl.

They tried searching in a second direction. Again, no luck. Portia hoped the girl wasn't intentionally abandoned. She looked down at the care taken to mend the girl's clothes and didn't think it was likely, but she grew up as an orphan, amongst other orphans, and knew how quickly things could change.

Just as they were about to turn around and try a third direction, a woman came running down the street, frantic, her eyes glued to the little girl.

"Justine!" the woman exclaimed, grabbing the little girl and swooping her up into a bear hug. The woman kissed the little girl all over her face until the girl was giggling and laughing, while the woman had tears of happiness.

The woman stopped fawning over her child, seeing Portia for the first time. "Thank you, thank you so much. She thinks it's a game to run. I usually catch her in time," the woman said apologetically. "Let me reward you." She was digging in her pockets and pulled out a few coppers.

Portia could see the woman was poor. She doubted she had any extra money. Any reward she gave Portia might mean not eating that night. Portia could not accept money from someone in that position. Besides, it felt good to prevent any child from being an orphan. No one should have to endure that.

"No, I won't accept it," Portia said firmly. She pushed the woman's hand with the coppers away, giving her a smile. She walked away quickly to prevent any further attempt at persuasion.

"Thank you again," the woman called after her.

Portia waved over her shoulder as she was walking away. Checking the sun again, it dismayed her to realize how late it had become. She increased her pace to a jog to get home.

The sun was just setting as she reached the front door of Elyas's home. She bounded up the steps until she came to an abrupt halt, noticing the front door was not latched. It was slightly open. An ominous sign, since Elyas himself had always cautioned her to keep the door shut and locked when she was home. The Warrens were not safe, he told her, and she was not to get careless, no matter that nothing bad had happened yet. There was always a first time—and he wanted her prepared. Portia's heart dropped at the sight of the open door. He would never have been that careless.

She pulled her dagger from its sheath and gingerly pushed open the door. It creaked while it opened, revealing a dark interior lit only by a fire. The kitchen table was turned onto its side, and at least one chair lay smashed on the floor. Legs stuck out from behind the overturned table. Portia realized the legs belonged to Elyas. A bitter taste of metal filled her mouth and she looked up to see that Mark was standing over him, his back to her, his arm raised with a knife.

Elyas must have heard the door. His legs twitched as he yelled to Portia, "Run!"

"No!" she yelled, shoving the door inward and running into the kitchen. Mark whirled to see her, and she recoiled in fright at the sight of him. A large scar ran diagonally across his face, just missing his left eye. It puckered, red and angry. His right hand held a dagger, but his left hand was missing two fingers. But the worst part of all was the look he gave her—it was full of hate, rage, and promised violence. This was not the Mark she remembered.

"Hello, Portia," he said, his voice a low growl. "Deyelna misses you."

10

"Mark," Portia said, "what happened?" Her heart broke just looking at him. Could she have shielded him if she had stayed?

"Life happened," he said, turning to fully face her. "I've come to bring you back. Deyelna is getting impatient, and you've been gone for far too long." He held up his hand that was missing the fingers. "Somehow she thought that hurting me would bring you back. But you never returned."

Portia wanted to vomit. Mark getting hurt was her worst fear—and she had let it happen. Portia shook her head. "I'm not going back. And you shouldn't either. You don't have to... you could stay here in Coverack. Or anywhere. You can get away from her." She said the last part with the plea in her voice.

Mark glared at her. He clenched his jaw and strode towards her stiffly. "I have no choice. I have to go back. And I'm not going back alone." He raised his hand and created a beam of light that shot out from it, hitting the ground at her feet, smoke bursting from the wood on impact. The smell of burning wood filled the air. Portia jumped back and ran into the room adjoining the kitchen, hiding behind a large over-stuffed chair. The light beam followed her, Mark controlling it as he walked towards her. She had never seen Mark do that magic before. From what she had learned from Elyas, it was clear that his magic pool was much stronger than hers.

The beam hit the overstuffed chair, and it burst into flames. Portia scrambled back. She conjured Mark's light mote magic and used her new skills to send them careening around the house, around Mark's head, and towards his eyes. Mark stumbled in surprise.

She used the light motes to harass and herd him to the front door. He resisted and wildly struck out with his light beam. Portia only just managed to avoid it as it passed over the walls and across the ceiling. She increased the number of light motes until all of Mark's energy was concentrated in batting them away from his eyes. Once she had Mark in the opening of the front door, she ran up to him and kicked his chest with all her strength. It sent him tumbling outside and down the front stairs. Portia wanted him as far away from Elyas as possible. She tried to use the light beam she had seen him create while continuing to send the motes swirling around his head, but her light beam was not nearly as strong as his. She managed to touch him with it, but his skin only turned pink. He easily scrambled out of the way.

Mark shook his head to clear the light motes, cursing at Portia under his breath. He formed another beam of light.

Portia redoubled her efforts—she had to stop him from aiming it at her. She looked around in desperation and saw a loose cobblestone kicked to the side of the street. While keeping up the light motes, she ran and grabbed the brick, quickly turned around, ran to Mark, and hit him on the head. His light beam stopped. His eyes rolled back into his head, and he fell to a crumpled heap on the street. Portia breathed heavily, still holding the cobblestone. She watched to see if Mark was breathing. Relief flooded her when she saw his chest rise. She hadn't killed him.

She looked around and didn't see anyone else on the street. Portia didn't want Mark murdered, no matter what he had done, so she dragged him by the heels to the alley that was thirty feet away and tucked him behind several bags of refuse.

She ran back into the house to see to Elyas. Her heart pounded when she saw the pool of blood surrounding him in the kitchen. She should have finished Mark off sooner and been back here to take care of him. "Elyas," she said as she fell to her knees next to him, trying to find where he was bleeding so she could stop the flow. "Don't leave me."

"You can't stay here," he said, so quietly that she could barely hear him.

"Don't talk. Save your energy," she said. His tunic was soaked in blood. She felt around frantically for his wound to staunch the bleeding but had a hard time finding it. There was too much blood to see clearly. He shook his head slowly no and grabbed one of her arms.

With surprising strength, he pulled her close. "Go... to the

Academy. Don't run... not again." He pulled her even closer. "Promise me."

Portia nodded, tears filling her eyes. She grabbed his hand with both of hers and pulled it to her cheek. "I will... just don't leave," she said. "Don't leave."

Elyas's eyes closed. His hand relaxed in hers. Portia sobbed as he died on his kitchen floor.

———

Portia didn't know how long she had stayed in the kitchen. She remembered staggering out carrying her bag and a small bag of personal possessions Elyas had kept. She didn't want to leave it for the thieves. She had checked inside, and it was mostly small objects from his daughter, Chenna, but it didn't feel right to let the neighborhood scavengers get them or toss them in the garbage if they were deemed not valuable on the black market.

She went to the linen shop and walked straight to the back room. She stripped off her outer clothes without a word to the shopkeeper, instead taking the bloody garments to the dyeing vat and tossing them in. It was late enough that all the girls were gone. Portia was grateful they didn't have to see her like that or know of anything that had happened.

She poured cold water on her clothes. The blood streamed off the material in the clear blue water. The shopkeeper came to stand alongside her and watched her work, waiting for her to speak.

Portia couldn't even bring herself to turn and look at him.

She felt numb from the inside out. The only sensation was a tingling on the top of her head and the ache of her hands in the ice-cold water as she drew the blood out. Elyas's blood. Her tears fell into the vat. "They killed him," she finally said.

"Him? Elyas?" the shopkeeper asked, pain and shock in his voice.

Portia couldn't bring herself to say anything further, nodded, swallowing the huge lump in her throat. "Oh, Elyas."

Portia knew the shopkeeper and Elyas had been boyhood friends. They made fun of each other to Portia, but she knew behind the jokes there was a deep affection. She felt even worse that she had robbed a person of someone they loved.

"Who did it?" the shopkeeper asked, concerned, as he glanced towards the curtain leading to the front.

"Mark... but not really Mark. He was under someone else's control," Portia said, and she stopped, realizing that the shopkeeper had no idea who she was talking about. It would be better to not say too much. "Someone from my past life. I won't be working here anymore. It's better for you. And it's better for me. I can't stay."

The shopkeeper nodded, bringing fresh linens over to Portia to help squeeze the water out of her now clean clothes. "You'll be missed, child. I know Elyas was happy having you there. He rarely talked about his daughter, but we all knew how hard it was for him without her."

Portia nodded, trying to concentrate on her clothes and not think about what had just happened. It was overwhelming. It hurt so badly, she was amazed her heart could still beat.

The shopkeeper walked to his desk in the back, opened a

drawer, and pulled out a small sack of coins. He grabbed several from the bag and returned to Portia, placing them in the sink where she was working. "Take these. Don't tell me where you're going. But I'm sure you could use this for a caravan ride or food, no matter where you will be. Elyas would have wanted you to have it."

"Thank you," Portia said, turning to the shopkeeper to grasp his hands in thanks. He gave her an awkward hug, patting her gingerly on the back.

Portia took a deep breath and then returned to her task. She shook out her damp clothes and put them back on with some difficulty since they caught on her skin and on her underclothes. It was uncomfortable to wear them this way, but at least they would dry. If she shoved the wet clothes into her bag, they would mildew and be ruined. She needed them for the trials.

She turned to see the shopkeeper staring at her. "Even I would not force you onto the street in wet clothes at night. You'll get sick. And if you get sick, Elyas will blame me, dead or not. Hang those clothes up to dry and rest here for the night. Good luck to anyone running through the Warrens looking for you tonight. I doubt we have to worry about them until morning. Leave then."

Portia had to agree with the shopkeeper. Leaving in the middle the night was foolish. And she was so tired, she didn't have the energy to argue. She took her outer clothes off again and hung them up while the shopkeeper pulled a goose down-filled pallet off the shelf and unfolded it, laying it on the shop floor. He threw down two heavy blankets on it, then he left through the curtain to lock the front and shutter the windows.

Portia lay down on the pallet and pulled the heavy covers over her. She shut her eyes, quickly drifting into a troubled sleep. She did not hear the shopkeeper pull out his chair and sit on it, feet propped up on the desk, a wooden rod across his lap, ready for anyone who might try to break in that night.

Her nightmare came back that night, stronger than ever. This time, something was lurking in the pitch-black void of the rent in the sky. She struggled to make it out in the dream but could only see gray and black shadows moving in the void —enormous shadows. She awoke, heart pounding and sweat drenched. For a moment, she forgot where she was and looked around wildly. Her eyes met the shopkeeper's concerned eyes as he still sat watch from his chair. "Nightmare," she said, not wanting to explain more.

He nodded then motioned for her to lay back down. It was still dark outside, too early yet to leave. She did so and fell quickly back to sleep, grateful he was there.

In the morning, she awoke to the smell of cooking bacon and eggs. Her clothes, now dry, were folded in a pile next to the pallet. She dressed quickly and wandered over to where the shopkeeper was cooking over the small fire in the back. The girls had not arrived yet for work, and the sun was still below the horizon, only a hint of pink and orange foreshadowing where it would appear.

The previous day's events came back to her in a rush. She swallowed bile at the thought of Elyas's death, as well as all that Mark must have gone through after she had left. She wished that Deyelna had never become a part of the Black Cats. Before she was leader, it had never been that ruthless.

Portia accepted a plate of food from the shopkeeper and ate ravenously. She didn't know what time the trials started that day, nor was she even sure where she was supposed to go exactly. She was anxious to get going and get to the Academy grounds early. She didn't want anything, no small detail, to get in her way of getting in. Now, it wasn't just for her but also for Elyas. She wasn't going to waste the opportunity he had gotten her.

She said goodbye to the shopkeeper and left before the girls arrived for work. The streets were empty, the dew heavy on the ground. She was grateful she did not have to spend the previous night outside hiding from Mark.

While walking to the Academy, she pondered what magic she should use for the test. She wasn't sure of the significance of her being able to do more than one family type of magic. She didn't want to ruin her chances of getting into the Magic Academy, so thought she should choose one, and only one, to use. Mark's magic with lights, motes, and beams was the one that she was most familiar with. It made the most sense to then use that one. Hopefully, it would be enough. She didn't know if they gave second chances if you failed the first time.

By the time she reached the outside edge of the Academy grounds, the sun was fully up, and the streets were crowded with students, hawkers, and others. There were visitors from all over the kingdom jockeying for a spot close to the gate and talking in excited whispers. Everyone was anxious about the day's events to come. Parents pushed children clutching their

Academy acceptance letters towards the gate. She pulled her acceptance letter out of her bag.

Portia got in line, jostled by the surrounding crowds. When she got to the gatekeeper, he took her acceptance letter, scanned it, and handed it back and motioned for her to follow the others into the grounds. There were Academy staff everywhere on the grounds. They were easy to pick out in the crowds—all of them wore dark blue robes. They guided applicants in one direction and parents in another. This was a test for the applicant's eyes only.

The first hurdle for Portia and all the other applicants was a physical. Colored orbs were flashed in front of her. She was timed on how quickly she called out their color. The test seemed easy, but she saw at least one applicant turned away when they could not get the color correct. He had burst into tears, but she could not stay to see what happened since one of the Academy staff members pushed her towards the next test.

The next test was a group endurance test. Cones were set out on the lawn a set distance apart. They were instructed to run between them from one line of cones to the next at the sound of the official horn. The intervals between the horn blasts would get smaller, but the runners still had to reach the goal cone before the next horn sounded. If an applicant was too slow and didn't reach the cone in time, they had to leave the test. The others would continue until no one was able to run fast enough. Portia lined up with a group of five other applicants. A staff member motioned for her to drop her bag along with the other applicants' bags beside the test field. She refused. She could not afford to lose anything that was within the bag. She would pass while carrying it, she thought, gripping her fists at her side, determined. The staff member shrugged and let her go on.

The officiant held up her hand to start the test. She got in the ready position along with all the others. The horn sounded and they raced to the first cone. They were all so overeager that all six got there long before the horn made its second noise, and they had to wait for it to sound again before running to the next set of cones. As the test continued and the horn sounded over and over again, it became more difficult for Portia to keep up. She wasn't the first to drop out, thankfully, but she did not make it in time after eleven soundings and was motioned off the field by a referee. She stood there, hands on knees, panting. Luckily, she had done well enough to pass the test. She was motioned into a final group gathered before the main Academy building.

Portia and the other finalists eyed each other, checking out their competition while they waited for further instructions. After several tense minutes, a man wearing long dark blue robes strode out of the main building towards the group. His wide grin and funny spiky hair were a sharp contrast to the serious faces of the applicants. The man held his hands together, waiting for them to be quiet and pay attention. Finally, all the applicants noticed that he was there, and the conversations died off.

"Welcome. You have all passed the initial hurdles. Congratulations. Now the *real* testing begins. Just getting here, to this point, is a privilege most in the kingdom will never know. So, for that, you should feel proud of yourselves. But even more so, I do understand that it would be heartbreaking to not get to the next level. So, pay attention closely. These instructions will not be repeated." He stopped talking for a moment and made eye contact with the applicants. Portia felt that he had somehow looked at each person individually, checking for something, then moving on. It was unnerving. She wondered if it was some sort of magic.

"Each one of you," he continued, "will draw a lot. A small stick with a colored end." He held up a stick with a red dot on the end to demonstrate. "Once you draw your lot, you will be directed to join others of the same color for your trial for acceptance into the Magic Academy." The would-be students started to mutter. He motioned for quiet. "Don't worry. All the tests are similar. No one color will have an advantage over another color. We just need a way to split you up into manageable groups."

Portia could tell that not everyone believed him. But there was nothing anyone could do but go along with it. She could tell by the sour faces around her that others had reached the same conclusion.

When it was Portia's turn, she drew a stick with a blue dot on the end. The Academy staff member who had held the sticks motioned for her to go join the other blue dot applicants. This group was congenial, smiling at her when she joined them. At least they would all have the same chance of getting in.

After all the lots were drawn, the groups walked to the

main building. Each group entered a separate classroom, the doors marked with the color of the group for that room.

Portia gazed around the classroom in awe. She had never been inside one before. There were rows of desks and chairs—at least thirty—lined up facing the front where a much larger desk sat facing the class. Behind that large desk, the entire wall was a chalkboard. She saw traces of writing on the board that had been erased before they got there and longed to know what it had said. She hoped this was not the only time in her life that she would be in a classroom. Schooling was a luxury orphans did not normally get.

She wiggled in her chair and checked out the desk. She spread her hands along the top of the smooth wood surface, imagining it was her desk, that she was a regular student here.

Looking around at the other applicants, she noticed they were not as impressed as she was. They sat at their desk stoically, ignoring the surroundings. Nothing seemed new to any of them. Her stomach tightened at how much more experienced than her they must be. What other experiences had they had, and she had not, that would help them pass the trials?

The door to the room opened in a whoosh of air. Portia had not seen anyone touch it. A man walked in wearing the same full robes as the one outside had been wearing, the one who had explained the lots. This man had long dark hair and a long face. He was the opposite of the man outside, whose bright smile had welcomed them to the trials.

"Hello, all. I am Professor Aelric Terfel," he said as he walked to the main desk and dropped his keys there, then turned to stare at the class. "Professor Terfel is my formal address, but if you pass the tests presented today, you may address me as Professor Aelric or simply Professor. How you get that privilege is as follows: In a few moments, we will all go outside, and there you will do your best to defeat me." The class muttered in response. This was not what they had expected. "You need to battle a professor into submission, and for a few lucky ones, the professor you will be battling is me. I will tell you right now I do not let subpar applicants into the Magic Academy." He stared intently at a boy in the front row who slid down in his seat, his face scrunching up. Portia willed the boy to not cry. She did not like this man. She did not like bullies.

Professor Aelric looked around, examining each face. "Are there any questions?" He gave a few seconds for anyone to answer, and when they didn't, he waved his hand in dismissal, "Good. It's better to not waste time now. I will answer the questions of those who are left after the trials. I don't expect it will be many. Follow me out," he said, picking up his keys once again and exiting the door.

Portia stood, waiting to join the crush of students leaving the room. She vowed to be one of the students remaining, just to prove that unpleasant man wrong.

He led them out to a gigantic arena behind the main building. There were square outlines of color on the grass about ten feet wide per side. There didn't seem to be a rhyme or reason to the colors—shades of red, green, yellow, and blue. Some squares had a student in them from the other color groups. Professor Aelric motioned his group towards a block of empty squares. The students filed over to them, each student selecting an empty square and tentatively stepping inside. Portia peered at the grass to see what the color was from, but it flickered in and out of her vision when she tried to stare at it directly. She guessed it must be magic of some sort.

Professors, all dressed in the same long dark blue robes, walked amongst the colored squares, occasionally stopping to enter one and face the waiting student inside. Portia tried to watch one such encounter between a professor and a student when her vision was blocked by a blue robe. She looked up to see Professor Aelric standing in front of her. He was so tall that he stared down at her.

"Hello, lucky one," he said, giving her a smile. Portia couldn't tell if he was mocking her or not. "I am a difficult professor, but fair. If you can disorient me enough in this challenge to touch me, I consider it a win on your part. Do you understand? You can use magic anyway you see fit."

Portia swallowed nervously. She didn't know what to say, so she only nodded.

"Begin," Professor Aelric said. He immediately raised his right arm, drawing up a wall of ice between Portia and himself.

Portia breathed a sigh of relief. At least he had not started out with an attack. She knew she could melt the wall of ice with her light. She concentrated on the spot between the two of them and saw him immediately stare at it. To distract him, she set off light motes blinking all over the wall, regretting she hadn't started that way.

But Professor Aelric was not content to let her work her

magic unchallenged. Tendrils of ice grew from the wall towards her, running along the ground quickly to her feet. Portia danced to the side, dodging the first tendril that raced towards her. She upped her power output to light, trying to make them brighter, so he couldn't see her and aim so accurately at her with his ice tendrils.

It worked—somewhat. The ice still raced towards her, but it was not as well aimed. She increased her concentration and output for both the melting ice and the light motes. She could feel her energy draining from her. Her magic pool was not that strong, but she had already accomplished more than she would have been able to without her endurance training with Elyas.

Portia ran to the ice wall to see if there was a hole melted yet or if she could push through with her hands. It was still solid even though water was pouring down the ice wall. She despaired that she was going to fail this test. She thought of Elyas and gave her magic all the energy she could muster, falling to her knees.

Suddenly, the light from Portia and Professor Aelric's square increased dramatically, blasting out wide across the arena. Students and professors alike turned to see what was causing it. Other battles halted. A few professors came running.

Portia didn't notice. Her eyes were closed in concentration as she pushed harder than she thought possible. She had a hard time breathing—her lungs did not want to work. The water from the wall pooled at her feet. She pushed at the wall with both hands. Ice tendrils grasped her feet. She ignored the stinging pain, pushing harder with her magic until her heart pounded in her ears. She shut her eyes tight against the light that was leaking out towards her from the other side of the wall.

"Halt!" Professor Aelric called over the wall. "Cease what you are doing!" Portia stopped her magic, her heart full of dread and disappointment. *No.* She had not broken through the wall.

The wall itself suddenly disappeared from beneath Portia's hands. She fell forward, no longer supported.

She looked up. Professor Aelric was no longer standing on the other side but instead was on his knees, shielding his eyes with his hands and weaving unsteadily. He sat back and slowly uncovered his eyes. He stared at her. She realized his face was pink with sunburn where his hands had not covered it. The look he gave her was dark. She did not know what it meant.

"Please give me another chance," she said. "I know I can pass." Her ears burned, feeling embarrassment as other students and professors heard her begging. She heard a student titter behind her.

Professor Aelric held up one hand, stopping her from saying another word. "You think you failed?"

"I... I didn't touch you," she said quietly.

Professor Aelric ignored that comment, instead staggering to his feet. Portia rushed over to lend a hand. He yelped when she touched his arm to steady him—his arm was sunburned from her magic.

"I'm sorry..." she said.

He waved away her apology. "What is everyone staring at?" he said, looking at all the gawkers that had come to see what had happened. "Go do your tests." The crowd stared. "Go!" he said again, his voice rising in volume. The crowd broke up reluctantly, going back to their own squares, leaving Portia and Professor Aelric alone.

"You didn't fail," he said as he examined his beet red arms.

"I didn't?" Portia asked, confused. "But I didn't touch you..."

"No, no," he said with a growl, "you passed. I had to stop you before real damage was done. Your magic touched me quite enough, young lady."

She passed! Portia could not believe it was really happening. She had passed her first magic test! Now she could be a student here and belong—so different from living on the streets and stealing to survive from day to day. For a split second, she wondered if it was a trick and she was being played with, but she pushed back that thought. They would not be so cruel.

Professor Aelric waved his hands, sending ice out in front of them. Portia watched a three-dimensional ice reconstruction of the school form on the grass. "We are here," he said, pointing to the map representation of the arena behind the school. "Go to this classroom in the main building. That is the next test in the process."

"Next test?" Portia asked, fear in her voice. Had she not secured admission after all?

Professor Aelric noticed her reaction, gave her an irritated look. "Don't worry, you've passed the important test. We just need to know what sort of magic you have—and how much—so we can place you in the correct house."

Portia breathed a sigh of relief. She wanted to thank him again, but he had already walked off while gingerly touching his arms and face, sending thin bits of ice over them. She could hear sighs escape his lips as each cooling bit of ice touched fiery red skin. Portia felt remorse at causing him pain.

But she found she couldn't linger on that thought; after all, it wasn't intentional. Her mind could not be kept from the magical fact that she passed. She had passed!

Portia walked to the main building to find out her fate.

11

Portia walked towards the main building and joined other students going in the same direction. She turned and looked to the arena. Most of the colored squares were now empty. Some applicants were walking out a side exit of the arena, one that led around the building, instead of heading towards its entrance. She felt bad for them. None of them looked happy—she guessed that they had failed the trials. She hoped they would have another chance in six months.

When they got to the entrance of the main building, they were greeted by an older student. His robes were also blue but not as full nor as long as the professors' robes were. His robe also did not have the hood hanging off the back that the professors' robes had. He smiled, waiting for the group to gather around him.

"The next test is to see if you have a single ability or skill for an entire tree of magic. You will all have the same core classes. But you will be individually assigned practicums based on the results of today's tests. We want you to be as strong as possible in your specific magic, and that includes finding the breadth of its extent, as well as exercising it for a strong depth," he said.

Portia wasn't sure she understood everything he was saying. She looked around at the other students. No one seemed confused. She decided not to ask any questions. She didn't want to stick out as ignorant.

"Please go into the building and follow the signs for the open classrooms. If the first room you encounter already has a student in it, just go to the next classroom. If all classrooms are full, wait in a line outside for your turn. We ask that there just be one student in a room at a time." When no one moved, he continued, his voice a little gentler. "It doesn't matter which room you're in. Go on." He waved towards the building.

Portia headed towards the building, one of the first to go. She found a seat in the second classroom near the front. She looked around nervously at the empty classroom. Perhaps she should have waited outside and let someone else go first.

Professor Hilda Griffiths entered the classroom. Her eyes widened when she saw Portia. Portia also startled, recognizing Professor Griffiths from the tavern in Holne. Portia wondered if Randall had gotten into the Academy six months ago.

"I recognize you," Professor Griffiths said, "but I can't quite place from where." She examined Portia closely. Portia wiggled under the scrutiny. She knew she looked different from how she had six months ago—better in most ways—so it was surprising the professor recognized her.

"I think we met at a tavern," Portia said, loathe to mention anything more specific. She wasn't sure why she was so shy.

"Ah, yes. I remember now. You were the hungry one," Professor Griffiths said with a smile. She pulled out two chairs facing each other and motioned for Portia to move to the one in front of her. She sat down, waiting for Portia. "Congratulations on passing the trial. Otherwise, you would not be here."

Portia nodded thanks. She sat down across from the professor.

Professor Griffiths took a small crystal globe out of her pocket and dangled it by a thin thread. She moved the globe between Portia and herself. "Use your magic on this globe," Professor Griffiths said, "and we shall see what you have."

Portia sent motes of light flickering in and out of the globe. Light fragmented in the crystals, sending rainbow colors all over the walls and ceiling.

Professor Griffiths inhaled, admiring the lights shooting about the room. "Beautiful, just beautiful. What else can you do?"

Portia concentrated on the globe, this time filling it with the soft golden light. It illuminated the room but was not strong enough to hurt their eyes.

"Very nice. What else?" Griffiths asked.

Portia realized she would keep asking until Portia ran out of things she could do. She did not want to share all of her magic with the professor. She was still unsure what it meant that she could do so many different things. A lifetime of protecting herself told her to reveal as little as possible. She created a beam of light, just as she had learned to do recently by watching Mark. She swung it around the room.

Professor Griffiths watched it with interest. "Again, very nice." She turned to Portia. "Anything else?"

Portia shook her head no. She didn't feel comfortable looking Professor Griffiths in the eye and lying. Hopefully she would just look shy.

"Okay. I think you have a skill for the tree of magic known as pyromancy, although your skill seems to be weak," the professor said, pulling out a piece paper from her robes and making a note on it.

Portia looked up in surprise. She didn't understand how her magic could seem to be weak considering how many people she had battled with it. Perhaps she didn't understand something about how magic worked. Maybe it had something to do with her ability to use different types of magic. That was not a question she wanted to ask Hilda Griffiths.

"Since you're a pyromancer, that means you'll be in my house," Professor Griffiths said with a gentle smile to Portia. "We will get to know each other much better. I am interested to learn more of how you got here from Holne and what has happened in the last six months. We'll have lots of time to talk about it."

Portia swallowed at that. She did not want to be under such sharp scrutiny.

Professor Griffiths took Portia's reaction as nervousness. She patted her on the knee reassuringly as she stood up. "I have other students to test. I'll send you on your way so you can get comfortable. I'm guessing new students will be filtering in for the next few hours."

Portia stood to leave, walked five steps to the door, then turned back to Professor Griffiths. "I don't know where I'm going." Her face turned red. Perhaps this was something she should have known.

"Not a problem. Here, let me show you," Professor Griffiths said, waving her right hand, creating a complicated map of lines of burning fire in the air.

Portia stepped back, feeling the heat from the map. She was distracted by the beauty of it, wondering how each line held in the air and didn't fall to the ground. Professor Griffiths's voice filtered into her ears. She realized she had missed half the instructions. Portia had to ask her to repeat them and forced herself to concentrate on the words and not stare mindlessly at the map. Professor Griffiths patiently repeated herself and waited for Portia to nod acknowledgment that she was ready to go before waving the map away again.

Leaving the main building by the side door, as she had been instructed, she found a small plaza. It had granite tiles paved in a circular pattern radiating out from a center spot in a spiral design. Along the spiral, there were different doors standing alone in frames without any supporting walls to hold them up. The doors were sprinkled around the plaza with no real pattern Portia could pick out. She walked closer to one to examine how it was standing up—the hairs on the back of her neck tingled from the magic that emanated from it.

Each door had a different symbol on it. Hilda had told her their house door had the etching of a small fire on it. It was the symbol they used in the school for pyromancy. The door she was standing in front of had an anvil on it.

She continued on, examining each door until she found the one with the fire symbol. She stood in front of it, took a deep breath, then reached out and knocked on it. Three knocks. On the third knock, the door swung in, revealing a large room. Much to Portia's surprise, it was filled with students talking and laughing and celebrating. The noise came out of the room and washed over her in a wave. It was a shocking contrast to the quiet of the plaza just a few seconds ago. Portia steeled her nerves and walked through the door.

Portia looked around the room. It was large—large enough to hold forty people or more. There were couches along three of the walls. There were no windows, only a few doors that were shut. Students sat on the couches or stood talking in groups. When someone noticed Portia standing in the room, they cheered for her, causing others to join in as well.

Before Portia could react, another student came up and pushed a glass of bubbly liquid into her hand. "Have a seat. Make yourself welcome," he said, gesturing to the sofas around the room.

Portia looked around more closely for an empty seat while sipping the sweet drink. The room was surprisingly crowded. Everyone in the room seemed to be her age or just a little older. One or two were as old as Peter and towered high above the others. The school was filled with young people.

A boy with messy brown hair caught her eye. He alone had noticed how awkwardly she stood there. He patted the sofa next to him then waved Portia over and pointed to the cushion once again. She nodded back and approached him.

"Come. Sit. We won't bite," he said. He gestured to the rest of the people sitting on the sofa. "We're all new this year too." His face turned red, and he quickly followed up his comments with more. "I mean, I'm guessing you are new. You don't seem as familiar with the place... I mean..." His face turned even redder.

The boy next to him had slicked-back hair that was white at the roots and faded to silvery blue at the ends. He was laughing at the red-faced boy next to him. Turning to Portia, he held out his hand. "Greetings. I'm Liam. The fool next to me is my brother, Richard. He means well."

Richard huffed and then finished his drink in one swallow. Liam ignored him, turning instead to point at the two girls on the other side of him. One was tall and willowy. Liam tapped this girl on her knee to get her attention, "Hey, we have a new one." Liam motioned to Portia. "Her name is..." He turned to Portia again. "What is your name?"

"Portia."

"Splendid name," he responded, "just splendid."

Portia turned a little red herself. She couldn't tell if he was making fun of her or really did like her name. The girl next to Liam wasn't laughing. That was a good sign. Portia gave the girl a small wave.

"My name is Ella, nice to meet you," the girl said with a sunny smile. "This one next to me is Mia." She leaned into the girl at the far end of the couch.

Portia was stunned at the brilliant red hair of the girl at

the far end of the couch. She'd never seen such fiery hair before. To top it off, the girl had red clothing and red boots. She was magnificently dressed. Portia suddenly felt self-conscious of her own clothing, even though it was new. The girl in red turned to Portia and gave her a gentle smile.

Ella leaned in towards Portia. "She doesn't say much, but I have managed to pry from her that she's from House Kelynack. A real noble. Isn't that cool?" She motioned to herself. "I'm just from a small town. How about you?"

Portia wasn't ready to answer that question. She took a sip of her drink to buy time, but Ella only stared at her with big eyes and awaited her response. Portia tried to sound casual. "I'm from a small town too." She looked around the room, searching for another topic. "Have you been here long? In this room I mean. I thought I was one of the first groups to pass."

Liam interjected. "Not too long. It's amazing how many students they can get through in a day. Richard and I thought we were amongst the first to finish too, but when we got here it was nearly full. Hopefully we can learn that sort of magic too while we're here. You know, getting a lot of stuff done without looking like it." He winked at Portia while Ella nodded agreeably.

Richard took Portia's glass along with Liam's and Ella's. Mia waved Richard away. He got up from the couch. "I'll see what I can do about refills."

"Good plan, brother," Liam said. He scooted closer to Portia once Richard was gone. "So, what did you think of the tests? I didn't think they were too hard. I was worried I'd be ravenous afterwards."

So, Portia wasn't the only one who needed food after magic. "I get hungry too!" Portia laughed, her shoulders relaxing a bit.

"Aha! I'll be right back," Liam said, getting up and walking over to a low table pushed against the wall. It was covered with sliced meats, cheeses, and breads. Portia realized how hungry she was when she saw it. Liam piled a plate high with food. He turned and winked at her, holding up one finger then grabbing a huge stack of bread to go with his plate. He came back to the couch and sat next to Portia. He handed her half the bread and then motioned for her to help herself to the plate he had placed on the couch between them. She didn't need a second invitation.

The sandwich she made was delicious. She shoved it in her mouth and took a bite so large that she could barely chew it. Just then, Richard came back with full glasses for everyone. Portia happily took hers. A warm feeling overcame her as she wolfed down her sandwich and held the glass of sweet bubbly liquid. Academy life was wonderful so far—a world away from her life a year ago.

The party continued on for another hour or so. Portia was overwhelmed with all the new people. A few of the older students came by—ones that had been in the Academy for a while—and introduced themselves to the new students. Portia was too exhausted to remember all their names. She vowed to do better in the morning.

Abruptly, Professor Hilda Griffiths burst through the door. She looked around the room, flashing a broad grin at everybody. She puffed her chest with pride, accepted a glass from one of the older students, and took a long drink, draining it. Giving back the empty glass to the waiting student, she turned to face the room. She clapped her hands loudly. "Hello? Hello. May I have everyone's attention?"

The talking in the room quieted down. Everyone turned to Hilda.

"Wonderful. Welcome to the Pyromancy house. You all have magic abilities in the same general magic tree. Some of you can even access magic on the whole tree of pyromancy, while others of you can only do one item, but often exceptionally powerfully. But regardless, it is our hope—we, the teachers of the Magic Academy—that by assigning you to live together, you can learn from each other. That is why we are divided by houses of magic." Hilda walked around the room while she talked, making eye contact with each student as she passed by. "That is not to say you can't learn from others with different skills. It is just that we believe you have the most to learn, and share, with others of the same magic tree."

Hilda stopped in front of a large door. "I'm sure that many of you are curious to see your new house. Shall we go on a tour?" When the students murmured yes and rose from their seats, Hilda nodded back then opened the door she was standing in front of and waved the students to walk in.

The first room they went into was the kitchen. Portia was amazed at the size of the room, as well as the size of everything else in it. There was an ice box that was at least seven feet wide. The hearth was enormous, having three spots to hang large kettles. There were long wooden tables and benches—

enough seating for thirty people or more—with large baskets on top holding fresh fruit. Onions and garlic hung in strings on the wall. Every surface was spotlessly clean.

In addition to the kitchen, there was a formal dining room with more long tables. Dorm rooms came next, each with a set of bunk beds and its own bathroom, complete with an installed bathtub. Portia did her best to hide her amazement. Perhaps all the students lived like this at home.

But the best room of all was the library. It was a large space with a vaulted ceiling. Comfortable, overstuffed chairs filled half the floor area with the other half dotted with tables and chairs. The walls themselves were made out of bookcases, each one packed from floor to ceiling with books. There were leather-bound books, sheaths of parchment tied together with string, and paper tubes stacked in a rack in the far corner. When Hilda was asked about them, she said, "They're maps, of course. You will all be expected to learn geography." Portia's heart leapt with excitement at that; she would finally get to learn about the world.

When they had run through all the rooms of the house, having gone up and down stairs and even explored the wash area in the basement and inspected the storage areas, they returned to the formal dining area. The students sat at the tables while Hilda went to retrieve the document with their dorm assignments. Her assistant had been working on it once all the tests were completed, finishing up while Hilda gave the tour.

Hilda returned from her assistant's office. "Now that

we've seen the whole house, are there any questions?" Hilda asked, looking around the room expectantly.

Ella held up her hand, and at Hilda's nod, she asked, "Yes, where are we? I remember opening a door in a courtyard, one that had many doors. But when I passed through the door, I'm suddenly in a huge house. Are all these houses somehow stuffed in the courtyard?" The other students laughed uncomfortably at her question. It was disconcerting to not know where they were, and even more so, to not have thought about it for the last several hours.

"That's an excellent question," Hilda said, nodding. "We are not in the courtyard. I do not know of any magic that is capable of squeezing houses into such a small space. The royal planners would give much for such skills." She gave a small chuckle, echoed by the class.

"Are we even in Coverack?" Liam asked with a chuckle.

"That we are," Hilda answered, her face suddenly turning serious, "but I cannot tell you where. We do this for safety reasons. I do not wish to scare you, but there are those who would rather that the knowledge of magic not be passed on. If they had their way, no young people would be educated in it." Hilda sat down heavily at the head of the main table. "Those doors in the courtyard are keyed to the inhabitants of each house. No one who is not in our house can get in here, at least not without special permission from myself or certain other Academy leaders. And that permission is rarely granted. The same is true for the other houses. You may be curious, but you will not see the interiors of the other houses without a good reason. So please, don't plan on any large parties—at least none that include outside people."

The room quieted at the mention of anti-magic sentiments. There were criers in the street predicting the end of the world and blaming it on magic and those with magical abilities. Portia had heard about a young child stabbed to death by his own father who believed that magic was the heart of evil in the world. Whispers reached her ears that the man was a part of a cult that was working to eradicate all magic. They preached death to those that defied them. The kingdom had worked hard to eradicate this sect but could never quite pin them all down. They would slip away from one town, only to reappear in another. It was a moving target for the royal guard.

"Yes, but how did we get here?" Richard asked, intent on the question and not seeming to share the same glum mood as the rest of the house. "I mean, how do the doors work?"

His mind was transfixed by the question. In every room in the house during the tour, he had been obsessed with how things worked. He had pulled on the cables of the dumbwaiter in the kitchen, inquired about plumbing for the bathtubs, and asked how the lighting system worked. The latter had been a wonder to most of them. There were the normal candles but also small glass bulbs that Hilda had said pyromancers could make glow, giving them all a gentle light. Portia wondered if the other houses were also so lucky, but she thought they might have other things that they did not, based on their own special skills. Or perhaps the houses shared magic between them.

"Portal magic is a very special tree of magic. A few planners for the Magic Academy have set up all the portals in advance. By decree, these portals can only be created with approval from the royal house. A practitioner of portal magic is rare. For safety reasons, it is important that any such skilled magician work with the royal house. We are lucky to have several of them in the Academy. Which brings up another rule—you are never to question what magical skills an instructor possesses. They will let you know what you need to know. Do not defy this rule." Hilda looked intently at all the students. Portia had never seen her have such a serious expression before. She was curious as to why but didn't dare ask it. Not even Liam was so brave.

"So, all the houses have access to their own portals. That is all you need to know about that for now," Hilda said, rising from her seat at the table, holding the parchment paper containing the room assignments. "It's been a long day. I'm sure you would all like to find your rooms. We start early in the morning, so it's important for you to get your rest."

Hilda read off names in pairs. The dorm rooms were small, approximately twelve feet square. They were large enough for the bunk bed, several clothing chests, and two desks—one for each student. Portia and Ella were placed in the same room. Ella's chest of belongings was already in the room. Portia was surprised at how large it was. It was painted with stick figures and crude images of children's toys. Ella shrugged when Portia asked her about it, giving her a smile. "My little brothers said they would miss me and wanted me to remember them. So, they painted my trunk."

The twins were placed together, of course, and Mia was given her own room since there were an odd number of students. Portia both felt sorry for her and a little envious. Privacy was nice, but Portia thought she would be too lonely if she had a room all by herself.

A gigantic eye peered down at her. Gray, patterned skin surrounded the eyeball. Long fingers appeared below the eye in the crack in the sky, grasping the edge of the tear on each side and straining to pry it open further. A screech filled the air. Portia couldn't breathe; her limbs were stuck in place.

She opened her eyes and saw the dorm room around her. She was tangled in the covers. She slowed her breathing, trying to calm herself from her nightmare.

The screech of a rusty hinge caught her attention as Ella came in from the bathroom, her hair bundled high on the top of her head and a sunny smile on her face. "You're awake, good. We have our schedules," Ella gestured to the desks, "and breakfast is in ten minutes. They rang the bell already."

"Bell?" Portia said, feeling confused.

"It's all on our sheets." Ella walked to one of the desks, lifting a piece of paper to show Portia. "They are customized for each of us. This is mine." Portia glanced over and saw that the other desk also had a small sheet of parchment on it. "They left us our schedules for classes. It talks about the bells too. We get a wake-up bell, and then a ten-minute warning for breakfast. I'm guessing they had to add the warning when some crabby elite student missed their first meal." Ella gave a little laugh. "You'd better hurry, or you are going to miss your own breakfast."

Portia leapt out of bed and grabbed her clothes on the way to the bathroom. Her stomach was growling. She was determined not to miss a single free meal.

The formal dining room was empty when they got downstairs. Continuing on to the kitchen, they found the rest of the house residents. The students chattered noisily over the sounds of silverware clattering on dishes. The smell of coffee overwhelmed Portia, and she left Ella's side to make a beeline for the kettle of the dark drink next to a stack of mugs. When she had a sip, she looked around to see what else was available. There were scrambled eggs, some fried meat, and a huge stack of pastries still on the serving buffet, even though most of the students had already gone through the line. Portia stuffed a pastry in her mouth and chewed it while grabbing a plate and piling it high with eggs.

She joined Mia, Ella, and several girls she recognized from the previous day's tour at one of the long tables. They were comparing their class schedules. Mia looked up at her. "What is your first class today, Portia?"

Portia pulled her schedule out of her bag. She scanned the paper. "History." She had not had time to read her entire sheet before breakfast. She regretted sleeping in so late, which also meant she didn't have time for a bath. She vowed to try out that tub as soon as possible, maybe even this evening.

"That's my first class too," Mia said. "Apparently we all have it together—at least those of us at this table." The other girls nodded in agreement.

Ella rose to get her own breakfast. She stopped by the table where the twins, Richard and Liam, were sitting. Portia saw her give them a hard time, punching Liam in the shoulder while laughing. She wished she had that easy confidence with others. It seemed so natural to Ella.

"The twins don't have history class with us," Ella said when she returned. "I forgot to ask what class they did have. I'll have to catch them at lunch." She sat down and wolfed down the eggs. Portia laughed a little. She might have found someone who ate even more than she did. "I also forgot to ask has how Liam gets that nice silvery hair. It's nothing like his brother's. It's some kind of magic. I know it is. Not sharing that trick is just criminal. I want to change my hair color at will too." Ella flipped her hair dramatically.

Mia laughed at Ella's determination. Her eyes met with Portia's, who had to laugh as well. Portia had known Ella for less than a day, but somehow she was sure Ella would get that information out of Liam.

When the end of breakfast bell rang, the girls rose and brought their trays to a rack at the end of the sink. There were slots for each tray. Portia wondered if they would ever meet the mysterious people who prepared their food and cleaned up after them. She felt a little guilty leaving her tray there for someone else to deal with.

They walked to class across the green lawn of the Academy campus. Portia, Ella, and Mia walked together, trailing a bit behind the other girls. Ella was waving to other students she saw as they went by.

"Do you know everyone on campus?" Portia asked, after Ella greeted yet another group of students.

"I'm getting there. I met most of them yesterday," Ella said while she retied her ponytail.

"Yesterday? During the trials? Weren't you a little distracted?" Portia asked, thinking about her own single-minded focus the day before.

"Yes, yes... the trials. I know I should do a better job of focusing, but there were so many *new* people. I just couldn't help myself." Ella gave Portia a sunny smile and a small rub on the shoulder.

Portia exchanged a look with Mia, who was laughing softly about it. The look Mia gave Portia indicated that she, too, had been concentrating hard on the trials. Neither one of them had made friends the way Ella had. Portia was suddenly glad that Ella was her roommate. She had a feeling she would get to know a lot of new people because of her. Her own social skills were not nearly as strong as Ella's.

Mia sighed as she pulled out her schedule from her bag to examine it. "I hate history. It seems like the only thing my tutor was ever interested in talking about."

"It is important to know what happened before," Ella responded sunnily. "Of course, I like all topics. I just like being here."

"I like being here too," Portia said without thinking. It was true though. She was excited for all the changes happening. She gave Mia a smile of agreement.

They reached the building indicated on their schedules. It looked older than the other buildings on campus, somehow fitting for the location of a history class. The cut stones of the walls were rounded with age and stained from rain. The roof looked older than all the other roofs on campus, having patches of green moss growing on it. Ivy covered the entire south face. Portia felt a tingle when she entered. She wondered how old the building really was.

Entering the classroom, they found around twenty other students already sitting at the desks. Professor Aelric was at the teacher's desk. He gave them a nod when they entered. Luckily, they found three seats close to each other and were able to keep chatting. However, their conversation was interrupted by a loud thud coming from across the room. The sound happened again. Portia looked over in the direction of the noise to see Magisend Lucy Gwynn of House Riddlepit glaring at her. Magisend maintained eye contact with her as she lifted a book then slammed it down on the desk. Soon, everyone in the classroom was staring at Magisend.

"That *student* is a thief," Magisend said through gritted teeth, pointing at Portia. "She should not be here. She should not be a student." Magisend slammed the book down yet again for emphasis then looked pointedly at Aelric. "House Adviser Aelric, do something about this."

Aelric looked taken aback at her demand. He glanced over at Portia then gave a grimace. Portia's heart sank at that look. She hoped her injuring him yesterday in the trials did not cause her problems today. She had not intended to do so. She thought she was following the instructions he had given her.

Aelric rose from his desk and approached the irate girl. "Please explain what is going on here, Magisend Lucy," he said.

"I caught that girl *in my bedroom* stealing my linens!" Magisend said, jabbing her finger in Portia's direction with each phrase. Portia slid down a little behind her desk. Mia and Ella looked at Portia, surprise on their faces.

Aelric's eyebrows knitted together in concern. He addressed Portia directly. "Is this true?"

Portia looked around at the other students in the class. They were staring at her, curious. Most of them looked as well-off as Magisend. They were probably nobles. Portia swallowed. Her stomach clenched.

"Student, when I address you, I expect you to answer," Aelric said, walking to Portia. He towered over her while she was still sitting at her desk. Portia looked at Ella's reassuring smile then back at Aelric. His face was dark. He was displeased with her.

Portia pulled herself up, sitting up straight, then lifting her chin high. She had magic just as all these other students did, which meant she had a right to be there. She didn't want to start off her new life with a lie. "Yes, Professor."

"Yes, Professor, what?" Aelric asked. He crossed his arms.

"Yes, Professor, I was a thief. I'm a commoner, not from any noble house. I stole to eat," Portia said quietly, her face turning red, despite her determination to not be ashamed of herself. Her ears burned when she heard giggles from some of the students. Ella reached over and touched her on her arm. Portia glanced at her. Ella looked warmly at her.

Professor Aelric raised his eyebrows at Portia's candid confession. He motioned for the class to be quiet, then nodded, thinking.

Magisend hit her desk, impatient, which drew a stern look from Aelric. She quieted, but her face was set in fury.

Professor Aelric uncrossed his arms and tapped his lip gently, looking at Portia. "You are, indeed, still a commoner. But by the decree of our queen, that is irrelevant here. However, while you are a student in the Magic Academy, you will not be a thief. Is that understood, Portia Harris?"

Portia nodded at him, the knot in her stomach loosening a bit.

"What! She is a *thief*!" Magisend said, leaping to her feet. "She should not be here! Not ever!"

Aelric turned to Magisend. "That is enough. I have spoken." His voice was loud and booming. Magisend sat down slowly, cowed. "What happens before students arrive at the Academy does not matter. However," he turned to face the class, "you are now, as students here, expected to follow Academy rules. Each house has a copy. Since this has come up already, I expect each one of you to have read the rules by tomorrow. You will be tested."

The class groaned in response. A few shot Magisend dirty looks for bringing about their first test already.

Aelric went to the head of the class and clapped his hands. "Now that excitement is over, let's begin learning, shall we? My class covers history. I would argue this is the most important class that you will have in your entire time at the Academy. I know some of the professors might disagree with that, but they are wrong. And you have my full permission to tell them so," Aelric said, giving the class a smirk. "You can learn all the strategy and all the magic in the world, but it will do you no good in this world if you do not understand where we have come from and the history of others. History shapes every choice a civilization makes. Whether conscious of it or not, it is in the bones of people to know where they have come from. It is much better to have this knowledge in your head where you can make conscious use of it. It gives you control."

Professor Aelric had the class's rapt attention. Portia had never heard of history being so powerful. She thought of Peter's obsession with it. Did he share that same thinking? Perhaps she should have been more curious about what he was reading when she was with the Black Cats instead of avoiding him because of his enforcer status.

She forced herself to focus on Professor Aelric's lecture. Now was not the time to think about the Black Cats. He continued. "Because of history's importance, this class is required for all students. And you must pass to complete your schooling here. If you do not pass it your first year, you will be held back from advanced classes until you do pass it. This is how important we all consider it."

This news was greeted with mutters from the students, which Professor Aelric ignored, barreling on with his lecture. "The most efficient way for me to teach this class is to know how much you know. I want everyone to raise their hands. When I say something that you do not know, I want you to lower your hand. We shall see how educated this group of young minds is." When no one raised their hands right away, Aelric waved impatiently for them to do so. "Come on, this history will not teach itself, although that would be a useful sort of magic." He muttered the last line.

Once everyone had raised their hand in the class, Professor Aelric started his lecture. "There are five human kingdoms, and many other nonhuman kingdoms." Everyone kept their hands up. Portia wasn't sure if she should, since she knew nothing of the other kingdoms, just whispers she had heard in the marketplaces. Occasionally, there were crates with strange curling scripts painted on the outside. These crates had come from far away, and the merchants who brought them guarded them jealously. Portia had never been able to see inside any of them.

"Okay, that's good. At least everyone here has some idea of the basics," Aelric said, pacing across the front of the classroom. "The first human kingdom that was settled was the Haulstatt Kingdom." A few hands went down. Professor Aelric nodded. "The first city that was founded was Coverack." Again, more hands went down. "The city was founded on displaced land, once having belonged to elves and dwarves." Portia lowered her hand at this, along with a few other students. She had thought that elves and dwarves were mythological creatures, stories made up to frighten children into behaving. She did not expect to hear about them in the capital—especially not in the renowned Magic Academy.

Professor Aelric continued. "Humans can be an aggressive lot. Just how aggressive, you will learn shortly. But humanity did not start on this planet. We were guests. Not very good ones if you ask certain kingdoms—many species would loudly proclaim that we have overstayed our welcome, if we were welcome at all. Regardless of that, the records say we came directly from the Well of Tears. Unfortunately, the records do not indicate how." A few more hands came down, including Ella's. Portia noticed that Magisend Lucy and Mia both still held their hands up. Magisend gave Portia a smug look, holding her hand even higher.

"One thing we do know, is that from the Well of Tears, humans traveled to the current kingdom of Haulstatt by boat on the rough seas. Many did not survive the journey. The records only list their names and tributes to them." A few more hands went down. Only the rich noble children still had their hands up. Mia was one of them.

Without thinking, Portia blurted out, "Where did they come from? Before the Well of Tears, I mean. We must've come from somewhere?"

Aelric was taken aback by the interruption but gave Portia an answer anyhow. "The Well of Tears is an island, we know that much. Before then is a mystery no one knows. That piece of information would've been useful to have in our records, but it seems to have been intentionally left out. Historians have been searching for hundreds of years for that bit of knowledge. No one has had any luck. In fact, no one can find the island itself anymore either." Aelric stopped pacing to face the class. "History speaks of past rulers visiting it to ask for knowledge from our ancestors." He looked off into the distance, a touch of longing coming into his voice. "A journey which I would very much like to take."

His lecture was interrupted by the bell for the next class. Ella and Mia gathered their belongings and filed out the door with Portia coming up behind them. Magisend stepped in front of Portia, separating her from her two friends. She leaned in close to Portia, careful to keep her voice low so Professor Aelric wouldn't hear her, "Watch it, *commoner*. You don't belong here."

Portia didn't say anything. She stared at Magisend, waiting for her to move out of her way. Magisend squinted at her, then huffed, finally turning and exiting. Portia exhaled then hurried to join Mia and Ella.

She was disappointed to learn that neither Mia nor Ella was in her next class, which was music. It was even worse when she arrived to see Magisend already there, surrounded by several other girls who all glared at her when she walked in the door. They must be from Magisend's house, Portia thought. One of the girls flicked a finger at her, sending the tiniest trickle of ice along the floor towards Portia's feet. When the teacher turn to greet Portia, the girl quickly banished the ice from the floor. She gave Portia a threatening smirk.

Portia's shoulders tensed as she sought out the chair closest to the door. She wanted to be as far away from those girls as possible. Most of that class passed in a blur. She was too distracted by the whispers and pointed looks from Magisend Lucy and her friends. They mouthed the words at her when she glanced over—*dirty thief* and *unworthy commoner* amongst others. Portia did her best to ignore them.

To add to her misery, Portia discovered she had zero innate musical ability. When they were listening to music samples, she couldn't seem to hear what the other students heard. Perhaps it was the constant whispers from the back of the room that interfered with her concentration. But there was no escape. Music was a required class.

The day did not get better when Magisend and the same girls were in her rhetorical class as well as her mathematics class. Both of those classes were so far beyond Portia's basic knowledge that she despaired of ever passing them. It would be even more impossible with the constant harassment of the girls from the cryomancy house.

After one of the girls had flicked a parchment ball at her head, Portia contemplated leaving the school. It would be so easy to walk away. Then she thought about Elyas, who had wanted the best for her. And how Mark was caught so deeply under Deyelna's influence that he would never escape the gang. At least not without help. And she couldn't help him if she didn't learn more and become stronger. She also thought of all the orphans in Valencia and the other cities who would never get a chance to learn news skills or attend the Magic Academy. Many of them wouldn't even live to adulthood. She straightened her shoulders, determined. She was not going to let these bullies drive her away from her hard-earned chance.

Finally, the last class of the day was over. Portia walked, exhausted, across campus towards the courtyard of doors. She was halfway across the field in front of the main building, a path that students used as a shortcut to the courtyard, when the ground beneath her and ten feet out in all directions was coated in a thick layer of ice. It happened so fast, she could not stop her forward momentum in time and slipped, her right foot shooting out from underneath her. She landed flat on her back, her head and back and legs stinging from the impact. She stared at the blue sky above her in shock. A gale of laughter erupted from behind her. It was Magisend Lucy and her friends.

Portia scrambled to her feet, struggling with the slick ice surface, which only made the girls laugh louder. Portia's face turned red with anger and embarrassment. She refused to turn and look at them. She wouldn't give them the pleasure of seeing how upset she was. Instead, she walked stiffly to the courtyard of doors. She quickly found the door engraved with the sign of fire and entered. The sound of the girls behind her disappeared as the portal worked, and she was whisked to her house. She exhaled with relief in the abrupt silence when the courtyard door shut.

She went to the kitchen to get a snack. Mia and Ella were sitting at one of the tables, each holding a hot steaming cup. Ella waved to her, motioning for Portia to come over.

"What have you there?" Portia asked when she was close enough for conversation.

"Chicken soup," Mia said, taking a step. "It's good. One of the older students said that they always have soup waiting for us in the afternoons. He said the teachers use it as a reason to not give any excuses for uncompleted homework. You can't say you were too hungry to work."

"I like that plan," Portia said, glancing at the pot hanging over the hearth. She helped herself to a large cup of soup and joined Mia and Ella at the table.

"How was your day?" Ella asked. "Mine was wonderful. I can't believe all the classes we get to take."

"Get?" Mia said, raising her eyebrows at Ella.

"How can you not like school?" Ella asked, her tone rising in surprise.

"Try having information shoved down your throat ten hours a day, every day of the week. I was hoping for a little more freedom," Mia said ruefully.

"You only had six hours today, so be grateful for that!" Ella chided. She turned to focus on Portia again. "Well?"

Portia sighed.

"That isn't a great sign. What happened?" Ella asked, concerned.

"I'm finding the classes really hard. I'm not sure how they think I can pass these classes—rhetoric, and mathematics, and music, of all things! I've never seen those subjects before."

"Oh, rhetoric is easy... it's just convincing people to do what you want them to do. It's a skill you need to have," she said, giving Portia a meaningful look. "We all do. I suggest you study hard in that one."

"I know someone who can do that with magic. It's awful." Portia said, thinking of Deyelna and her control over the Black Cat gang. She shook her head to clear the memory.

"Controlling people with magic would be great. I know some people I'd use it on," Mia said with enthusiasm, perking up. She looked off into the distance, imaging some scenario in her head. "I would use that all the time." Both Ella and Portia stared at her in surprise. This was not the quiet Mia they'd seen over the last day.

Portia sputtered out, "Now I'm glad you don't have that ability."

Mia's eyes refocused on Ella and Portia, who were still staring at her. "Oh, I wouldn't use it on my *friends*, sillies."

Ella nodded slowly. "Okay."

Portia turned to Ella. "The worst part of the day was getting hazed by Magisend and her cronies from the cryomancy house. They were in every one of my classes. Why couldn't I have had you two instead?" She leaned her hand on her chin, depression pulling over her.

"Oh dear," Ella said.

"They even turned the field into a skating rink just to see me fall," Portia said. "You heard Professor Aelric this morning. They might be able to risk breaking the Academy rules, being nobles and all, but I'm sure that I can't."

"That's awful!" Ella said. She gathered everyone's mugs, refilled them at the kettle, then brought them back. "I just can't stand bullies. There is no reason for it!"

"If only everyone thought that way," Portia replied.

"Well, they should," Ella said. Mia nodded in agreement. "I agree you can't directly fight them, but maybe you can give them a taste of their own medicine in a sneakier way... now to think of a way to do that."

The three of them sat at the table, silent, sipping their chicken soup. Portia was not versed in the ways of subtle power struggles. Everything in the Black Cat house had been direct—and brutal. Of course, it was possible there were currents of power she was not aware of. Regret gripped her belly when she thought that there might've been ways to do things better, to protect Mark better.

Ella sat up quickly. "I know. I'll teach you a trick I learned as a kid. It's perfect. You can set magic to be tripped later when you are nowhere in the vicinity." Ella gave Portia a conspiratorial smile. "I used to use it on a boy I thought was cute in the village. Thank goodness he never figured it out."

"Oh, that's good!" Mia said.

"I agree. As long as there's no way to trace it back to me," Portia said. "How does it work exactly?"

"It's called a node. You make a little pocket, I'll show you how, and you can set your magic inside of it and seal it back up. Once that's done, it's like a little present—perhaps not a pleasant one—for whoever trips it."

"How do you trip it?" Portia asked. "Can you send it for one specific person?"

"That I don't know," Ella said, then paused thoughtfully. "The village wood chopper showed it to me. He set his by location. Anyone who walked through a path would trip the magic. He used it to scare away large animals where he knew he was going to be working the next day. It was only to give them a little fright so he could work without worrying about being surprised. Or worse."

Portia considered that. "That might not be specific enough. Though if they follow me around all day like they did today, then I'll know easily enough where they will be." She looked at Ella with appreciation on her face. "Thank you.

That's the most helpful thing I've learned all day. Even if I probably won't use it. I don't dare."

"No?" Ella asked, her face falling.

"It's too risky," Portia said, "but I'd like to learn it anyhow, just in case things get really desperate."

"Great!" Ella perked up again, pleased and happy. "I agree that you have to be careful. I don't want to lose my roommate. But you should know this anyway, just to have something to protect yourself."

"Okay, that makes sense," Portia said amiably.

"Excellent. Let's practice this after dinner. I'm not sure what of your magic would be the best to put in a node, so we'll have to experiment." Ella said. Portia groaned again at the thought of having to concentrate even more that day, but she still nodded her agreement.

The girls clinked their mugs together to celebrate the plan.

The rest of the evening passed in a blur. Ella tried to teach Portia the node magic in their room after dinner, but Portia kept nodding off. Mia had already begged off due to exhaustion and retreated to her own room. Portia felt envy at that refuge, but since she didn't have a room of her own to retreat to, she sat cross-legged on her bed, struggling to pay attention to Ella's excited chatter. When she could not keep her eyes open any longer, she simply lay down and fell fast asleep. It took several minutes for Ella to notice.

That night, Portia's nightmare returned stronger than ever. It was different this time though. Now she could see the land below the cracking sky. It was an island in the middle of a rough and choppy sea. Storms and lightning agitated the water. The sea's waves tossed a fleet of wooden boats. One of the boats flipped over, its masts disappearing under the waves, only leaving the curve of the hull facing upwards under the flashing night sky. Then the hole appeared overhead, a spot clear of clouds, rain, or stars. The giant eye in the velvet blackness of the hole peered down at the island below. The wretched hands came into view, prying at the breach in the rent sky.

Portia woke in a cold sweat. Her bedding was soaked. She shivered in the cool night air. The nightmare now had details from her history class. She groaned. The more details the dream took on, the more frightening it was.

Getting out of bed, she changed into her nightclothes, feeling around in the dark so as to not wake up Ella. She struggled to sleep after that. She lay awake in her bed staring out the window at the full moon and thinking about Mark and Elyas. Her stomach hurt at the thought of the two people she had let close to her suffering like they did. She couldn't do anything to help Elyas now—she could only work hard to make him proud. But she might be able to do something for Mark, even if he didn't want her help. She would work hard in the Academy and learn enough skills to defeat Deyelna and protect Mark. She had to. There was no choice.

Portia got out of bed, careful to not wake Ella. She dug around in her trunk and found Elyas's bag. Its soft leather was comforting. Opening it, she pulled out the locket she had found of him and his daughter, Chenna. It was the perfect symbol of a loving family—something she wanted more than anything in the world. Crawling back into her bed, she held the locket close and ran her finger over the engraved face over and over again, imagining her face next to Chenna's and Elyas's on the inside.

Eventually, sleep reclaimed her before morning.

13

The next several months passed in a blur. Mia and Ella tutored Portia most weekends, helping her to catch up to the rest of the students. When they weren't available, Portia spent most of her time studying on her own in the library. Many of the books there could not be removed, so it was easier for her to study there, where she could read the heavy ancient tomes. Her favorite subject was history. Most of the history books were not even allowed outside of the air-controlled room they were stored in. Studying in that room had become one of Portia's favorite activities.

Winter had taken over Coverack. The campus was covered with a thick snow. Icicles hung off the buildings. Valencia had never been this cold—the sea air would never allow it. But Coverack was further north, and colder, even with the moderating effect of the sea. Portia was grateful for the coins from Elyas that allowed her to purchase a thick winter coat, a wool-lined cap, and a pair of sturdy gloves.

The winter was also excellent cover for the cryomancers to increase their harassment of Portia. She thought it must take less energy from them to create ice when the air was already so cold. It took more of her own energy to make the fire magic in brisk winter air. Portia longed for summer.

Magisend and her friends' favorite place to harass Portia was outside the library. Since Portia went there nearly every day, it was easy for them to lie in wait for her to come by. No matter how hard Portia concentrated on being alert for their tricks when she approached the building, they usually—but not always—managed to catch her by surprise with a sheet of ice under her feet. At least her falling technique had improved. She no longer had huge bruises on her backside, or a ringing head from it hitting the ground. She could now twist in air and fall on her side, her arm safely tucked in and not sticking straight out at risk of breaking. It still hurt to fall, but not as badly.

One especially cold morning, Portia was hurrying to the library to return one of the few books she had been allowed to take out. She had stayed up late the previous night reading the volume and so overslept that morning. Portia ran along the path running behind the library, the book tucked safely in her bag wrapped in parchment against the cold air. She didn't want to be late and lose her borrowing privileges.

Suddenly, the entire path in front of her turned to ice. The ice radiated out in all directions. It continued out and curved up into the air all around her. It formed a huge bowl with her in the center, trapping her. Nowhere was the ice a flat surface. Portia slipped and skidded up the wall of ice that had just risen in front of her, carried by the momentum of her running. She had not encountered this ice formation before. Once her forward motion ran out, she slid back down the wall, falling and landing with a thud on top of her bag. Her practiced falling technique did not keep her from crushing its contents. She yelped when she heard the parchment crumpling as she landed on it. Panicked, Portia pulled out the book and saw that its binding was broken on one edge, the pages hanging loose. Rage filled her. It was one thing to harass her. It was another to cause damage to the book and jeopardize her ability to use the library.

Portia heard the giggles coming from the other side of the ice wall. Her fists clenched. This was too much. It could not go on like this. She *had* to do something about their harassment before they decided they could do even worse things.

The girls from the cryomancy house were getting bolder. Recently, they had not been erasing the evidence of their tricks as quickly as they once did. They had left puddles of ice around Portia far longer than they had dared in the fall. Portia stood in the bowl of ice and waited for them to eventually relent and remove the ice they had put up around her. But the walls stayed up. The giggling voices disappeared. They had left her trapped in the ice bowl.

Portia growled in anger. She would have to get herself out. She breathed in deeply then created intense light on her gloves and boots and pressed them into the ice, melting it. Water flowed down the ice walls and pooled around her boots, entering through the laces and soaking her feet. The frigid water sent shivers up her body. She swore this would be the last time they did this to her.

The next morning, Portia created a duplicate of herself and sent it towards the library. She hung back far enough to not be seen but still close enough to observe what happened. She realized, chagrinned, that she should have done this much sooner. At least she could've learned the pranksters' favorite hiding spots.

When the duplicate Portia—and the real one tagging behind—got close to the library, Portia spotted the cryomancers hiding in the bushes next to the library. An enormous icicle hung down from the library roof, partially shielding them from view. But it glimmered in a funny way, partially invisible, giving away its magical source. It was not a real chunk of ice but the illusion of one. Standing under an icicle that large could be fatal, which is why no one would think to look for a person standing there. Portia admired the genius of this. But she also wondered if the illusion of ice was actually a cryomancer ability.

When the duplicate Portia got to the corner of the library building, a sloping wedge of ice rose underneath its feet, tilting sharply upwards and sending the duplicate falling and tumbling. Portia appreciated the impossibility of anyone to remain standing in that situation. She would've tumbled just as certainly as the duplicate had.

Portia was grateful that they had not created an icebox or other structure that hid the duplicate from her view. She was able to command her duplicate to rise and run back away from the library. When she and her duplicate were out of view of the hiding cryomancers, she released the duplicate magic, leaving only herself standing.

She returned to the library and made it inside, this time unmolested. She spent the day studying history, eating the sandwiches she had packed in her bag, and fully enjoying her favorite topic. She missed dinner back at the house because she wanted to stay until after dark. Luckily, the house cook was generous in letting her pack as much food as she wanted for the day.

Once it was dark, Portia left the library to study the cryomancers' hiding spot more closely. The fake, magical icicle was gone. The roof at that spot was two stories above the ground level. There was a lot of room below it. There was also an overhang that hung down past the building, leaving three or four feet of open space between the lower edge of the roof and the building.

Underneath that area, the snow was packed down from the standing cryomancers. This was clearly a favorite hiding spot—the snow was so compacted that it was nearly solid ice.

Portia had been practicing her own cryomancy skills that winter. She didn't want anyone to know she had that ability, but the constant snow on the ground and the occasional sleet that came down on warmer days were excellent cover for any ice that she herself created. Portia had taken advantage of this as much as she could whenever she had time between studying and tutoring with Ella and Mia. Now was the perfect time to use her new skills.

Looking up at the gap between the edge of the roof and the building, she concentrated on creating a solid block of ice.

Then carefully, creating a dense grid within that ice, she created small nodes of magic and filled each one with light energy. She wanted each node, when tripped, to release a burst of heat.

Then she placed a series of nodes, all under where the girls normally stood, but this time containing cryomancy—the magic of freezing. She wanted these nodes, when tripped, to freeze any nearby water.

When Portia was done placing all the nodes, she felt a bit faint and dizzy. It had been a long time since she had used that much magic. Even though the magic within the nodes would deploy later, she still had to use her energy up front to create it. She headed back to the house to rest.

The next morning, she headed back to the library. Gritting her teeth, she approached the spot where she knew the girls would play their trick on her. It was never fun, whether she knew it was coming or not. Regardless, she had to continue to implement her own plan. She walked to the spot where she always fell, and without fail, the ice appeared beneath her feet. She slipped and fell, concentrating on triggering the nodes in the ice over the girls on her way down. She wanted all of the magic to release at once.

Screams of surprise erupted immediately as a shower of water fell from above, soaking Magisend and her friends hiding below. Portia then activated the nodes beneath their feet. The girls' screams turned into cries of pain as the magic was released up, freezing the water around their feet, the water soaking their clothes, and the water in their hair and on their skin.

Professors and students walking on the campus grounds reacted to the screams and came running to see the cause. Portia struggled to her feet on the slick ice and saw a crowd gathering around Magisend Lucy and her noble cryomancer friends' hiding spot. Going closer, she caught a glimpse of the girls at the center of the crowd. Each girl was a nearly frozen lump of ice stuck to the ground, the ice in their hair joining with the ice covering their clothes and shoes, attaching them to the solid ice beneath their feet and surrounding them. Portia couldn't help herself—she giggled at the ridiculous sight. After months of pain at their hands, it tickled her to see them suffer from their own medicine.

Magisend's eyes found Portia. They glared at her from within the ice on her face. One of the surrounding students used fire magic to melt some of the ice on Magisend. Others quickly followed suit, helping to release her noble friends from their ice trap. As soon as Magisend's mouth was free she screamed, "Portia Harris, you'll pay for this!"

The surrounding students and professors turned to see who she was staring at. No one else was close to Portia, so it was immediately clear who Magisend was glaring at. Portia backed away, still unable to stop laughing, and turned to run.

Unfortunately, she ran right into a professor in blue robes who grabbed her by the wrist and held her fast. "What's this all about?" the professor asked, looking at Portia closely.

"I don't know, but it's funny," Portia replied. The look in the professor's face banished all laughter. A small lump of dread formed in Portia's stomach.

"We shall see how funny it is," the professor responded, a frown etched on her face.

Another professor grabbed Magisend. "You seem to be the ringleader of this group. We'll get the rest later if we need them."

The professors brought Magisend and Portia to the main building. They asked the receptionist for an emergency disciplinary board. The disciplinary board was how the school investigated any student wrongdoing. It was thought immediate resolution was better than letting things fester, especially in a school full of students with magical ability.

Portia and Magisend waited in a small room for twenty minutes while the board was gathered. Portia was not happy. She did not expect to get caught. She knew there was no direct proof. It was rather unfair that Magisend and her friends had been harassing her for months without repercussion, yet the first time she fought back she was hauled in front of a board. She could not lose her place in the school.

Magisend, for her part, simply smirked at Portia. Portia could see that Magisend's lifetime of being a noble in a high house in the city conditioned her to expect things to go her way. Portia looked away. That smirk enraged Portia. She concentrated on her breathing; she knew she needed to be in control of herself.

When they were brought into the small room where the disciplinary board was, Magisend and Portia sat in front of a long table that had Professor Aelric, Professor Hilda, and an elderly professor Portia had never seen before. The professors nodded at the students. Hilda gave Portia a look of disappointment. Portia didn't know if this could get any worse.

"So, once again, Portia Harris, I am asking you what happened?" Professor Aelric asked Portia.

This drew a look of irritation from Professor Hilda. "Why would you assume she knows? Perhaps it is a student from your house that is responsible?" Hilda said to Aelric, an edge to her voice.

"From what I've been told, my student was the victim in all this," Aelric retorted without looking at Hilda. "Portia," he continued, "I am expecting an answer."

Portia shrugged. "I don't know what happened. I fell down on ice in front of the building, and then I heard screams. I came over to see what the screaming was all about... I'm sorry if I thought it was funny. It's not funny when a student is hurt." She looked down, trying to look contrite. Thinking about the scene still made her want to laugh. She quickly thought about Professor Aelric's angry face to stop the giggling from bubbling up once again. It took physical effort to keep from smiling.

"See!" Magisend pointed at Portia. "She's laughing! She thinks it's funny. She did it and she did it maliciously."

"Enough." Hilda stared at both girls closely. "Portia, have you ever fallen in that spot before?"

Magisend jumped to her feet. "What does that have to do with anything? *We* were the ones who were hurt today." Magisend's voice rose with indignation.

"Student Magisend, I do understand that you feel attacked today, but you will respect the rules of this board. Do not speak again unless you are spoken to," Professor Hilda said in a stern voice to Magisend.

Magisend looked in appeal to Professor Aelric. He motioned for her to calm down. Magisend slowly sat down again, not happy.

"I have fallen there every day for months now. I told my friends about it. If whatever's happening is malicious, then I am a victim as well," Portia said.

Professor Hilda's eyebrows rose at the word 'months.' She had not heard anything about this, despite Portia being in her house.

"She did this. I know she did! This *commoner* does not belong here. She does not follow the Academy rules." Magisend crossed her arms, glaring at Portia. Professor Aelric put his face in his hands at Magisend's outburst. His student was not behaving well.

The third professor stroked his gray beard and contemplated both students. "Was Student Magisend not frozen? If Student Portia is in your house, Professor Hilda, then would she not only have the ability of fire?"

All three professors looked at Magisend and Portia. This fact was true. As a student of the House Pyromancy, any ice abilities should be out of reach for Portia.

"Could this have been someone else from your house?" Professor Hilda asked Magisend.

"No. They wouldn't dare cross me," Magisend responded.

"That is an interesting answer," Professor Hilda said. "I hope this does not mean you are bullying them." She gave Magisend a meaningful look.

Professor Aelric answered for Magisend. "Of course, she's not bullying them. I would not tolerate that in my house. They are well educated girls who have full respect for the House of Riddlepit and Magisend Lucy's family. She has simply come to expect that from her peers."

Aelric's answer did not sit well with Hilda, but she made no retort.

"I want the truth cube used. I know my rights. I want this student proven guilty and then expelled!"

"Let's not jump to consequences just yet, young lady," Professor Hilda said.

Aelric looked pained at Magisend's demand. "Is this really necessary?"

"I'm afraid it is," the third professor said. "We cannot find the truth, clearly, from asking these two students. We shall have to use the cube. Perhaps it will point us to another party who is guilty."

The third professor rose from his seat and went to a cabinet behind him. He pulled out a small crystal cube the size of an apple and brought it to the table in front of them. He set it down in the middle of the three professors.

"What is this?" Portia asked. She had never heard of a magic cube.

Professor Hilda answered her. "It is a truth cube. It cannot force you to say anything. However, if you speak a lie, it will tell us by changing color. We power it," she motioned at herself and the two other professors, "with our magic."

The three professors concentrated on the cube. It glowed a gentle yellow-white. It pulsed slightly.

"Since Student Magisend Lucy has brought the accusation. We will begin by questioning her," Professor Aelric said.

"Why me? I'm innocent," Magisend said defensively.

"It is the procedure," the third professor said with a gentle nod towards Magisend.

Magisend huffed at that, crossing her arms.

"Let's start with something easy," Professor Aelric said, then turned to Magisend. "Student Magisend Lucy, are you a member of the House Cryomancy?"

"I am."

The cube did not change colors.

"Do you bully any students in our house, the House of Cryomancy?" Aelric continued.

"I do not," Magisend responded without hesitation. The cube faded in color, turning a faint pink color. Magisend glared at it. Hilda's eyebrows raised a fraction.

"Have you ever retaliated against a student who said something negative about the House Riddlepit?" Aelric asked.

"I have not. I do not need to," Magisend responded. The cube turned from pink to red, the red intensifying until it was a deep burnt umber.

The red light reflected on Professor Aelric's face. He was surprised at this response. He hesitated, formulating what question to ask next.

Hilda fumed. "Student Magisend, do you know anything about why Portia falls on ice every day?" she asked, jumping into the silence.

"Professor Aelric Terfel is asking questions, not you," Magisend said. Professor Hilda frowned at this response.

"But you will answer this question anyhow, Student Magisend," the third professor said, an edge to his voice. He leaned over his templed fingers, awaiting her response.

"Of course I don't!" Magisend said.

The cube stayed red. It pulsed strongly. It did not return to the gentle yellow that indicated truth telling. Magisend's face blushed a deep red, nearly the same color as the cube.

Portia marveled at Magisend's folly in calling for the truth cube. She just had to find a way to survive its questions herself. She never would have pulled that prank on Magisend if she had known she would have had to face this.

"Interesting," the third professor said, looking meaningfully at Aelric. Aelric slid down in his seat a little, looking for just a moment like a chagrined student himself. The third professor turned his attention to Magisend again. "I feel I must remind you Student Magisend that the penalty for lying to members of the Magic Academy, faculty or student, is likely far higher than the penalty for playing a prank. This applies to all, even those of a high house. This kingdom depends on magic users. It needs its magic users of the highest quality, those that it can trust. Liars are not trustworthy, a truism that I hope is obvious to you."

Portia swallowed at that. She did not have the House of Riddlepit to hide behind. There was nothing to protect her if she was caught lying.

14

Portia faced the three professors staring at her expectantly, her throat dry. She had lied, and they would soon find that out. Her stomach hurt at the thought of being turned out from the school, or possibly worse. But there was nothing she could do about that now—she had to face whatever consequences were coming towards her.

Professor Hilda spoke first. "Student Portia, did you cause the events this morning?"

Portia nodded slowly. "I did not cause myself to fall. I did, however, do things to Magisend and her friends." Portia's stomach jumped in anxiety. Her face burned red. She looked down, unable to face the professors in front of her. The cube shown a gentle yellow. She was telling the truth.

Silence hung in the room. Finally, the third professor spoke to Portia. "Who helped you?"

"No one."

The cube remained a warm yellow.

Aelric sighed in exasperation. "That was clearly cryomancy. Someone must have been helping you."

More silence. Portia stared at her fingernails, resisting the urge to bite her cuticles. She shoved her hands under her legs to keep from fidgeting.

Hilda said gently, "Speak. We must know."

"No one helped me," Portia said. "One of my housemates showed me how to make magic nodes months ago. But that is it. She knew nothing of what I did this morning. She would not agree to it or help to do it. She's too nice."

"Liar!" Magisend said. All three professors looked at Magisend. Aelric motioned to the cube—it glowed yellow, the color of truth telling. Magisend slumped down in her seat, muttering.

"Portia, can you do more than pyromancy?" Professor Hilda asked Portia.

Portia nodded.

"Speak, child," the third professor said. "We need to hear you say it."

"Yes, I can do more than pyromancy. Please don't throw me out for lying about it," Portia pleaded, fear breaking through her control. "I just wanted to belong here. I didn't understand the penalty was so high for lying."

The three professors shook their heads in shock. Hilda spoke first. "Portia, that is not something we will kick you out for. It is a precious ability. Although lying is serious. Never do that again."

"If it's true about her skills," Aelric said, dropping some of his earlier embarrassment. "We shall need you to prove it. It would be bad if you were lying about *that*."

Portia nodded. The third professor motioned for Portia to begin. Portia created a three-dimensional map of the campus from ice. She heard a gasp behind her from Magisend. She banished the ice map, replacing it with a map of fire. She let it burn for a moment, heating the room, then banished it as well. Finally, she created ten duplicates of herself, crowding them around the professors' table.

The professors looked around at the duplicate Portias, amazement on their faces, until the third professor looked back at the real Portia, who was still seated in her chair, and nodded. "Enough. We get the point, young lady," he said.

Portia banished the duplicates.

The three professors stared at Portia.

"Anything else—no, don't show us, just tell us," Hilda said, holding up a hand to stop Portia from using any more magic.

"I can heal myself, a bit. It's why I can still walk after all those falls," Portia said, finally glancing at Magisend, who had been the architect of her pain. "I can do a few other things too." Portia shrugged her shoulders. "Once I see someone else do a type of magic, I'll try to do it myself. Sometimes it works."

The three professors stared at Portia, their mouths hanging slightly open. Aelric was the first to recover, closing his mouth and sitting up.

"How are you sustaining all that magic at the same time?" the third professor asked.

Portia shrugged again. "It doesn't feel that hard. It's not like at the entrance trials where I had to use a lot to make the lights bright and hot. It's easy to make the lights, or anything else, but it's hard for me to make it very intense. Someone else might've been able to make enough magic to freeze water around the entire library. It took a lot for me to make the nodes just for the corner."

The third professor nodded at this information.

Hilda looked at him questioningly. "So, she has an incredibly wide magic pool, able to do nearly anything, but it's just not that strong?"

"So it would seem," the third professor answered. "It's not unusual to not have strong magic, but as we all know, such a wide magic pool is incredibly rare."

"Yes, if this is true, she would be the third in our entire history," Aelric said.

Magisend huffed and said spitefully, "You're kidding right? You don't really think this *commoner* is a Jack of Magic, do you?"

Hilda eyed Magisend, all of her patience gone, "It looks that way, Student Magisend Lucy Gwynn of House Riddlepit. And we have you to thank for bringing it to our attention, so thank you." Hilda nodded at Magisend.

Magisend glowered at the three professors and Portia but said nothing more. Professor Aelric stood, taking hold of the still glowing cube, and waved over it. The glow dimmed until there was no light left, leaving the cube dark. He put the cube back in the cupboard from which it came then returned to his seat. "Student Magisend, I must ask that you not repeat anything you have learned here. Not to anyone. Not within our house. Not to your family," Aelric said.

"Sure," Magisend said, resentment in her voice.

"Just to be sure, we will use an oath binding spell on you," Hilda said.

Before Magisend could protest, the third professor held up his hand. "Standard procedure. For everybody."

"What about Portia?" Magisend asked.

"If it wasn't for that cube, no one here would know," Portia said.

Aelric gave a grunt of dissatisfaction but did not disagree with her.

"I won't tell anybody. I can't be brought here again," Portia continued. She didn't know of a way to counteract the cube. She was sure no one would show her, even if it was possible.

"Then I suggest you stay out of trouble," Hilda said, giving Portia a wink to soften her words. "Your silence won't be required for long. We need time to consult with others... such as the royal family."

"You're going to talk to the royal family about her?" Magisend asked.

Portia almost felt bad for her. She could sense that Magisend thought this was the worst possible outcome. Not only was Portia a commoner, but she was important enough in her own right to be brought to the attention of the queen. Even Portia herself found the thought of scrutiny by the royal house a little nerve-racking.

"She should know," the third professor said, looking at

Portia seriously. "There is more than one reason we require your silence, Student Portia."

Portia swallowed nervously. This did not sound good.

The professor continued. "There are things we have not taught you yet, this being your first year at the Academy. The first is that the occurrence of a Jack of Magic, if indeed Portia is one, has a great deal of significance. We need to consult with the royal advisers and historians." He cleared his throat, leaning into Portia to emphasize the next point. "The second, and perhaps more worrisome, point for you is that there are those who would kill you if they could, if they knew your abilities. Despite the best efforts of the Royal House, not all are believers of magic being necessary to our safety." He stood, indicating the review was over, then nodded to Aelric and Hilda and exited.

Fear ran down Portia's spine. *Kill?* The professor was worried about her safety on the campus. She had thought being here was the safest place she could be, but perhaps the opposite was true—it marked her as a possible target. Being a Jack would make her the primary target. Portia felt a little dizzy.

"Is he talking about those idiotic anti-magickers?" Magisend said, unimpressed. Portia turned to her, surprised at her reaction. Magisend was either very brave or very stupid.

"Magisend," Professor Aelric said, a warning in his voice.

Aelric and Hilda themselves rose. They each pulled on delicate chains around their necks and pulled out small keys hung from them underneath their robes. Moving to a huge metal cabinet in the corner behind where they had been sitting, they each placed their key in a keyhole and turned. The cabinet would only open with both keys present and used at once.

Aelric pulled out a small wooden box and placed it on the table in front of where Magisend stood. He opened the box and withdrew a large silver disk and lay it on the table. "Student Magisend, please place your right palm on this disk."

She looked it suspiciously. "What is that?"

"It is an oath binding channel. It is here for just such occasions, so we don't have to wait for an oath binder to arrive."

Magisend didn't move.

"Student Magisend, this is not optional," Professor Hilda said gently, "but it will not hurt. You will still remember what occurred today."

Magisend slowly placed her hand on the disk.

Aelric and Hilda said a few words quietly in unison. Portia's neck tingled. The magic they were using was strong enough for her to feel where she was standing. She was glad she did not have to submit to it. They finished and nodded. Magisend quickly withdrew her hand.

"Go back to your houses, you two. Remember, no one is to know any of this," Hilda said. She pushed the two students towards the door.

Portia and Magisend walked through the halls of the main building in silence. Neither one was willing to let the other go ahead, so they walked in parallel. They reached the outside together, exiting into the cold winter air.

Portia glanced over at Magisend and saw that Magisend's clothes were still damp. She felt sorry for her. The air was cold, well below freezing, and Magisend did not have a magical ability to warm herself. Her cryomancy was not that useful in the wintertime.

Magisend noticed Portia looking at her and retorted in a chilly tone, "I don't care what skills you have; I still don't like you."

Portia stopped feeling sorry for Magisend. "I don't like you either. But we are in the school together. Perhaps we could at least be decent to each other."

Magisend did not respond at first. Their steps crunched through the brittle layer of ice over the snow, ice that had formed from melting under the warming sun during the day. After several minutes, Magisend responded, "I suppose." She turned towards Portia and grabbed her arm, forcing Portia to face her. "But you owe me for my linen."

Portia shook her head at that. How could this wealthy girl be so petty? That linen was so far and above anything she could ever afford. It was not as if Magisend had paid for it out of her own pocket. She wrestled her arm free and continued walking towards the courtyard of doors. Magisend fell in step with her but did not press the subject further.

They reached the cryomancy door first, and Magisend entered without a word to Portia. Portia stood for a moment alone in the courtyard, the magnitude of the day's events just settling in her brain. She gave a sigh, then turned towards her own door. She wouldn't be able to tell Ella or Mia what happened, but their faces would be a comfort, nonetheless.

Portia felt odd, exposed, now that Professor Hilda and Professor Aelric knew about her magic. It sounded like a good thing, but perhaps it wasn't. Perhaps she was a mutant they would want to control and contain. Was she being naïve to trust them? Her upbringing on the street told her the smart thing to do was to run away, to hide. But nothing that had happened in the school gave her any reason to distrust either Hilda or Aelric. As grumpy as Aelric might be, he was always true to his word. But then again, neither one of them had said having such a wide magic pool was a good thing, only that it was unusual.

Portia watched her feet crunching on the snow, crossing the paths around the spiral. She liked to cut across rather than following the twisty path between the door.

Suddenly, a dagger blade appeared out of the left corner of her eye and swung towards her throat. Portia jerked back, raising her arms in defense. Turning, she saw Mark staring at her, a look of hatred on his face. Behind him, she saw Peter and Deyelna. Deyelna was dressed in all black leathers, and her face was stiff with hatred. All three stood between her and the door to the pyromancy house.

15

Portia stared in disbelief at the trio in front of her. Deyelna was the most unlikely part of their presence. What was she doing outside of Valencia? Portia knew Mark was deep under Deyelna's spell, especially with Deyelna right there, but what about Peter? Was he there by choice?

Portia backed up slowly. "What are you doing here? How did you get on campus?" If she could get Deyelna talking, it might buy her some time to the pyromancy door. The door would not allow them to follow her—if she could just get through it. It was not keyed for Deyelna, Peter, or Mark. They would be barred, and Portia would be across town, in the house at its secret location. But that door was useless to her if she couldn't reach it.

"You thought you were safe at some secret location, didn't you, you horrible brat," Deyelna said, venom in her voice. "I told you I had a plan. And friends in high places. I'm not just a *gang* leader. I'm going to take over the whole city of Valencia... just as soon as I deliver your head."

Portia circled around the group, trying to get closer to the pyromancy door as Deyelna talked. But she must have been too obvious, because Deyelna narrowed her eyes at Portia, then signaled to Mark.

Mark raised his hands, casting his magic light motes towards Portia. She squinted to reduce the glare then made a dash around Mark, wanting to get some distance from him. He turned with her motions and increased the intensity of his magic. The light became so intense that Portia could barely see, stumbling as she ran, and looking through slitted eyes.

Peter ran to intercept Portia, his hands outstretched to grab her. Portia saw his dark shape coming her way and veered away just in time. Peter's fingertips brushed her. Portia glanced back towards the pyromancy door and saw Deyelna guarding it, standing in a fighting stance. Somehow Deyelna knew which door she was trying to reach.

Giving up on the door for now, Portia veered away, evading Peter for a second time. Mark's magic was making it difficult to see, and the heat from his lights was melting the snow under their feet, making it slick. Portia ran away from the courtyard of doors, her traction improving the further she got from Mark's lights. She was grateful to realize that he had not learned the skill of casting them as far away as she could, the skill that Elyas had taught her. If she could get some distance from Mark, she could escape the bright lights of his magic.

Deyelna let out an enraged yell of surprise as Portia ran

away from the trio. Portia ran between the two closest buildings to the courtyard, pushing her way through the deep snow between them, trying to get out of sight. She could hear all three of them pursuing her.

Portia turned the corner of the first building. She stopped, struggling for air and then looking around to see if anyone was on the campus grounds nearby. There was no one. No one to help her. But then again, no one to see her use her magic. And she needed all of it now, even the magic that wasn't pyromancy.

Looking at the path between the buildings behind her, Portia threw up an ice wall to stop her pursuers. She took a few breaths more then heard the cries of anger as they reached the wall of ice. A glow came through, an intense hot glow that Portia knew must be from Mark's magic; he was melting the ice. Steam billowed up and around the sides of the wall as the powerful light evaporated and melted the ice on contact. If he was able to use that light beam on her, he could kill her. She had to get more distance.

Portia concentrated on Deyelna. She wanted to stop Deyelna most of all since Deyelna was more than likely controlling the other two. She envisioned a block of ice encasing Deyelna's feet behind the wall. It took a lot of Portia's energy, but she gritted her teeth and concentrated on the magic until she heard Deyelna's exclamation from behind the ice wall; she must have succeeded.

Suddenly, Peter appeared at the top of the wall, his head poking out of the steam and quickly followed by the rest of him climbing to the top of the wall. Portia stopped working her ice magic on Deyelna and ran. Peter saw her and leapt down, chasing after her.

Portia berated herself for being so slow at working her magic. Her breath came in ragged gasps as she struggled to put distance between her and Peter, her legs struggling with the deep snow. Portia could hear Peter gaining on her from behind, his feet crunching through the ice and snow. Peter's long legs easily overtook her. She sensed, more than felt, the rush of air as Peter swung a mallet at her. Portia ducked just in time and felt a whoosh of displaced air as the heavy weapon continued past her right cheek. A second later, a blast of light went by her right cheek as well—Mark had broken through the wall.

"Watch it!" Peter yelled behind him to Mark. Portia glanced back to see Peter nursing a singed arm where Mark had struck him with the light. While Peter yelled at Mark, Portia created a wild slope of ice underneath Peter's feet. She made the ice a series of waves—nowhere was it flat. Peter yelped once again as his footing became unstable, sending him crashing to the ground.

Portia looked up in time to see Mark aiming his light at her once again. Deyelna was nowhere in sight. The ice at Deyelna's feet must have held. Portia ducked, evading the light, then took off again, away from Mark and going between another set of buildings. She found an evergreen bush still thick with foliage even in the depth of the winter and hid behind it, waiting for Mark to appear.

When Mark came around the corner, Portia held her breath, waiting for him to come closer. When he was even with the bush, she grabbed him by the arm just as he passed by. She pulled him into the bush alongside her with a yank. She wanted to be alone with him without being discovered by Peter or Deyelna.

Mark careened into her, a look of surprise on his face at his target suddenly becoming the hunter. Portia tried to recall how Deyelna worked her magic. Mark grabbed Portia's arm back, the look of rage returning to his face. He pulled at her, trying to get her out of the bush. Portia resisted. She knew she had to work quickly. She attempted Deyelna's magic of persuasion on Mark, trying to use it the way she thought Deyelna had done. Mark stopped pulling on her arm, a look of confusion on his face. But he still looked enchanted, his eyes vacant. Portia's efforts had some effect, but not the right one. She needed to cancel Deyelna's magic, not force him to do another thing. She didn't want to control him the way Deyelna had.

Portia tried again, but this time she concentrated on voiding Deyelna's magic and sending it off into nothingness instead of trying to imitate it. A flicker of recognition came into Mark's eyes when he was looking at her then disappeared again. This time, Portia had the right idea, but her magic wasn't strong enough. She had to put more power into it. Summoning all the strength she had, from the tips of her fingers down through her legs and feet, Portia poured her energy into voiding Deyelna's magic. She felt Deyelna's magic resisting, pushing back. Portia tried harder. Then, suddenly, Portia felt a snap in the air. Vibrations hit her skin as the air molecules around her recoiled from a burst of magic as Deyelna's magic broke, sending Mark's hair flying back in the burst. Mark stared at Portia, his look softening from rage to recognition. His gaze returned to what she remembered from their time together in Valencia. She had done it—she had broken Deyelna's spell on Mark. He was back.

He looked stunned at his present circumstance, looking around the campus, at the snow, at Portia. "What is going on? Where are we?"

Portia pulled him fully back into the bushes, hiding them from view to buy a few minutes. "We're in Coverack. You came here with Peter and Deyelna to get me." She grabbed his arm with both of hers, pleading, "Help me."

Mark's confusion resolved into a look of pain. His face scrunched up. Portia recognized the look; it was the one he always had when fighting tears. "I don't understand. I can remember doing horrible things, but I don't know why."

"It's not your fault, it's Deyelna," Portia said. Snow crunched at the top of the path between the two buildings. Portia peeked out and saw Peter then turned back to Mark. "Please, help me fight off Deyelna and Peter. I can't go back. I think they want to kill me."

Mark winced at the word kill. He glanced up and saw Peter coming towards them. "I will help you. But I won't... kill. I can't do any more terrible things."

Portia's heart ached for Mark. She nodded. At least he was back. At least he would help her.

Peter ran towards them, his eyes trained on the bush. Portia glanced at the wall behind them. She didn't want to be trapped against the brick wall. But the two of them could probably take Peter. It would be better to be on the offensive.

Portia grabbed Mark and pulled him out of the bush along with her to face Peter alongside her. Peter stopped running, his face twisted in surprise to see Mark facing him in a fighting stance. Portia and Mark exchanged glances then bolted towards Peter. Portia wanted to capture him and disable him so they could deal with Deyelna and find out why they were there. She was tired of running. She was tired of being attacked. She had to find out what was going on and, if at all possible, put an end to it.

Peter stared for a second at Mark and Portia. Then, where there had been one Peter, now there were two. Another one had stepped away from the original and stood beside him. It was impossible to tell which one the real Peter was and which was the duplicate just by looking at them. Portia and Mark each faced off with the closest Peter. The two Peters turned and ran.

"I'll get one, you get the other," Mark said, running after the Peter who had been closest to him. Portia didn't bother responding except to run after her own. They needed to engage them before Peter thought to make more duplicates, if he was capable of doing so.

Portia glanced to see how Mark was doing in time to see Mark raise a hand and shoot a light beam towards his Peter. The light beam went straight through him. Now Portia knew she had the real Peter. She returned her focus to the Peter running in front of her, increasing her speed as much as possible. The snow made it difficult.

The Peter she was chasing turned to face her holding two long knives. She had only seen one knife on him earlier—one of the two knives he held was a duplicate. Deyelna did not carry long knives like that, nor did Mark. Portia instinctively pulled out her own knife from its sheath at her waist. She was painfully aware of how much shorter it was than Peter's, not to mention his added reach from his long arms.

Peter ran towards her, attacking, before she had time to use magic instead of physically fighting. He swung with both knives, his arms coming together to trap her between the blades. Portia twisted sideways, leaning back and escaping the path of one blade. She was not so lucky with the second one. The blade sliced through her thick jacket and undershirt and cut deeply into her right arm. Portia's right hand lost its grip on her own blade. She felt the sting of the wound and grabbed her arm to stop the bleeding while dodging further away from Peter. Peter turned to her, ready to attack a second time, raising his arms to repeat his double swing. Portia stumbled back and lost her footing, landing on her butt. She kicked her feet on the ground to scramble out of the way.

Peter made another step towards her but was knocked off his feet as Mark tackled him from the side. They tumbled in a blur into the deep snow, Mark furiously attacking Peter and keeping him from Portia.

Portia looked down at the blood from her arm. It covered her jacket and was falling into the snow beneath her. The blood was coming too quickly. She closed her eyes for a second, concentrating on healing her arm the way she had healed the tree. The magic was slow, sluggish. It did not want to be used the way she was trying to use it, but it relented, finally. The stinging in her arm subsided, replaced by a strange twinge. Opening her eyes, she removed her left hand to examine the wound. There was a white zigzag scar on her arm, but no bleeding. She breathed a sigh of relief.

Portia concentrated on Mark and Peter. They were rolling around so fast, it was hard for her to pick out one over the other. Finally, Mark pinned Peter beneath him, one hand on each wrist holding down the blades. Peter bucked widely underneath him. Peter outweighed Mark, and Portia knew Mark could not hold him for long. Not wasting time to stand, she raised both hands and sent a river of ice towards Peter. She concentrated on it covering his legs and his torso, and finally his hands. She did not cover his face and mouth. As terrified as she was, she did not want to kill him.

Deyelna came around the corner, breaking Portia's concentration. Deyelna's boots were dark with water. She must have found a way to melt the ice encasing her feet. Her eyes were black with fury. They were trained on Portia. She held two short daggers out in attack position as she ran towards Portia.

Portia scrambled to her feet, running away from Deyelna and towards Peter and Mark. She hissed at Peter as she got closer. "Stop attacking us. It's in your best interest."

He looked at her with angry eyes, his lips pressed thin.

"I could freeze you completely. Completely," she said, motioning to his mouth.

His eyes opened wide in understanding. He quickly nodded agreement. "I'm not the only enforcer, Portia."

Portia ignored him, turning instead to concentrate on Deyelna who was still running towards them. Portia sent ice out towards Deyelna's arms to knock the blades out of her hands. Deyelna stopped running to duck sideways. The ice missed her completely. Deyelna gave Portia a look of contempt and a small laugh before running towards her again.

Portia sent a wider band of ice, one that would be more difficult to avoid, towards Deyelna. Deyelna ducked again, but the ice grazed her this time. It hit her on the shoulder and knocked her sideways. Deyelna lost her grip on one of her blades, dropping it into the snow. It disappeared. Deyelna growled.

"Surrender," Portia said, mustering as much authority as she could. "Your enforcer will do nothing. You cannot win."

"Never, you foul little thing. How dare you defy me," Deyelna said, her voice low and gravelly.

"You have no authority here," Portia said.

"I'll always have authority over you, *Black Cat*."

"No!" Portia said, shooting another tendril of ice out and knocking the second blade from Deyelna's hands. "I'm no Black Cat."

Mark came to Portia's side, ready to attack Deyelna. Portia shook her head no.

Deyelna's eyes widened in surprise at Mark's actions. She glared once again at Portia. "You think you're above the rules. No one is above the rules. Not my rules."

"Surrender," Portia said. "You will never control me." Portia just wanted this over. Her arm was throbbing, and exhaustion from the battle was sinking in.

Deyelna yelled incoherently as she ran towards Portia.

Portia scrabbled back to avoid Deyelna, intending to knock her down when she got closer. But Deyelna reached into her jacket and pulled out another knife. Deyelna gripped the knife tightly, twisting her body to stab at Portia, who instinctively parried then hit back, realizing too late she still had a dagger in her hand. The blade sliced into Deyelna's stomach with a sickening ease. Portia gasped in horror.

Deyelna fell back, the weight of her body pulling at the knife still in Portia's grasp. Portia didn't think to let go of the blade, so she was still holding it and drawing it out of the wound when Deyelna fell. The moment the blade exited, blood spurted out from Deyelna's stomach. Portia dropped the knife and dropped to Deyelna's side. She placed both hands on the gushing wound to stop the blood. It didn't work. Blood oozed out from between her fingers, covering her wrists and flowing down Deyelna's body to pool in the surrounding snow.

Portia had never mortally wounded anybody before. Her head felt dizzy with panic. She could feel Deyelna's heartbeat weakening. Less blood came out with each pulse.

She finally thought of her magic. She closed her eyes, shaking with panic and exhaustion, and tried to concentrate on healing Deyelna's wound. She felt, through the magic, inside Deyelna, but it was confusing. She wasn't sure exactly how to heal her. She kept trying anyhow, blindly working. Deyelna stopped breathing. *No, no, no.* Portia desperately shifted her magic to Deyelna's lungs, but they did not respond. Then, Deyelna's heart stopped beating. Portia tried to force it to restart. It would not. Deyelna died underneath Portia's hands.

Portia opened her eyes and sat back in shock. She had never wanted to kill anybody. Not even Deyelna. A strangled noise came from behind her. She turned to see Mark looking at her, wild-eyed. Peter glared at her.

Portia tried to clean her hands off in the snow, the blood sticky and thick. Water crystals stung her hands as she rubbed them into the snow, leaving blood on the white expanse. Tears filled her eyes.

She got to her feet, staggering. She walked over to Mark. "Are you okay?"

He nodded back at her that he was, then look down at the ground, uncomfortable.

"Stay here, with me, in Coverack," Portia said quietly.

"I can't. You don't understand," he answered, refusing to look at her.

"At least don't go back to Valencia."

He nodded. "No, I can't go back there. Not after..."

"It doesn't matter to me," Portia said. "It wasn't—"

"It matters to me. It matters to me. I should've been able to do things differently," he said, a tinge of anger creeping into his voice. He scowled at the ground. "I need to be a different person, a better person. I need to find that within myself."

"Deyelna controlled you. You didn't do this."

"But she did it so easily. And I did those things. It was my hands." His shoulders shook a little. He turned his back to her, hiding his face.

Portia didn't want him to feel defensive. She softened her tone. "Maybe in the future you will find me again."

He nodded. "Maybe." He straightened his shoulders then turned and gave her a nod. She would have to be satisfied with that for now.

Portia's heart broke at the awful life Mark had been dealt. Guilt wracked her for not trying harder to get him away from Deyelna. She opened her arms and gave him a hug. He was stiff at first then slowly relaxed and gave her a hug back. "I'll always be looking for you. I'll always want you to come back." She gave him an extra squeeze and then released the hug.

Mark looked down, then said hesitantly, "Portia, be careful here. Deyelna was working with some dangerous people in Valencia—I don't know who—but they got us on campus today. They created a distraction on the other side of the grounds to pull away the guards. They were giving her power, but in return, she was supposed to deliver you."

"Me?" Portia asked, incredulous. What could they want with her? They couldn't know about her being a Jack—she had just found out herself. She turned to glare at Peter. "Does he know about this?"

Mark nodded. He motioned to Deyelna's lifeless body. "What should we do?"

Portia turned and looked at the body. She could claim self-defense, but what reason would Mark have for being there? There was no good story they could give that would keep him from being stopped by the guards. They would throw him in prison—and maybe worse. Portia wanted to keep him from that fate. She owed him at least that much. "Go. I will tell them the truth, that I was attacked. They won't know about you. I promise." She motioned for Mark to go.

He did not move. "I can't..."

"You must," Portia said, pain in her voice, "Please, for me?" He hesitated, then finally relented when she motioned again. He ran down between the buildings and away from Portia, who stood between Peter, still frozen to the ground, and the dead body of Deyelna of the Black Cats.

16

Portia watched Mark go, her heart sinking with each step he took away from her. Finally, he turned the corner, passing out of her sight.

The sound of metal hitting metal behind her caught her attention. She turned to see Academy guards dressed in blue uniforms peering between buildings, their shields out and swords up. She called out to them and waved to get their attention. They came running towards her between the buildings, looking from side to side to make sure it wasn't an ambush. She'd seen guards before but didn't realize there were so many on campus, or that they had swords.

The lead guard caught up to her. He was well over six feet tall and towered over Portia. He surveyed the scene, seeing Peter caught in the ice, and then noticed Deyelna's body. He motioned for the other guards to surround Portia while he went to investigate the body. He felt Deyelna's neck for a pulse and confirmed that she was dead. He bowed his head for just a second then raised it, looking at Portia with narrowed eyes.

Returning to Portia's side, he said roughly, "Did you do this?"

Portia nodded slowly, swallowing. "They attacked me. I was defending myself."

"Are you a student here?"

Portia nodded again.

"You do understand, don't you, that we can get to the truth here?" the guard asked Portia, giving her a meaningful look.

"I'm not lying. These two attacked me. I didn't... I didn't mean to kill her. It was an accident," Portia said. She hoped the guard wouldn't find out that she was from the pyromancy house. If he knew that she was from that house, then he would know there was something off. She should not have been able to freeze Peter to the ground.

The guard looked at the large number of footprints in the snow then at Portia once again.

"Who else was here?" he asked.

"Only these two," Portia said. Then she locked eyes with Peter and continued, raising her voice to be sure Peter could hear her. "There was no one else."

The guard eyed her skeptically but did not press further.

Two of the other guards were using light magic to melt the ice around Peter. They had freed his arms and hands, which were red with cold, and were now working on freeing his legs.

The lead guard approached Peter. "Is this true?"

Peter looked away sullenly. He rubbed his hands gingerly as if they hurt.

"I expect an answer," the lead guard said, an edge in his voice.

Peter refused to look at him. The guard crouched down to Peter's eye level, forcing Peter to look at him. "Is this true?"

Peter finally nodded.

"Is there anyone else?"

Peter shook his head no. The guard stood then motioned for the two working on freeing Peter's legs to continue. Once Peter was free, the guards helped him to stand. He was unsteady on his feet. Another guard brought chains and shackled Peter's feet together.

Portia watched it all. She glanced back at Deyelna's body and then down at her own hands. There was still blood around her fingernails and on the sleeves of her jacket. Portia felt a little ill. Her stomach hurt. Suddenly, blackness crowded around her vision and she felt light-headed. Before she knew it, the ground was heading towards her face. She was fainting.

A guard caught her before her head hit the ground. He gently eased her down until she was lying on her back in the cold snow. Portia's vision improved a bit, but she was still seeing spots. She felt nauseous.

The lead guard came back to her and peered down at her. "Are you hurt?"

"No," she said weakly. "I was, but... but I fixed it." She held up her healed arm for him to see.

One of the other guards brought all the gathered weapons

from the ground and laid them at the feet of the lead guard. There were at least five knives, two of them streaked with blood.

The lead turned to Peter. "Which one of these knives did you use?"

"The long one," Peter said. He looked down then said quietly. "It's poisoned."

The head guard motioned to the largest guard in the group. "Get her to a healer now. Bring the knife too."

A burly guard rushed over and gently picked Portia up. Portia was not small, but she felt tiny in his arms. A second guard followed holding the poisoned knife. The burly guard picked gingerly through the snow pack, each step sending shoots of pain through Portia's head as she laid in his arms. She looked up at the light blue sky, foggily thinking it too beautiful a day to die. Her stomach knotted in nausea and then blackness overtook her.

PORTIA REGAINED consciousness inside the healer house. She was lying on a tall platform in the main ward. The two guards were still there, conversing with a healer dressed in all white. Snow from Portia's clothing was melting on the table. She had not been there long.

"We don't know what happened, exactly," the smaller guard said. He held up the long knife. "We do know she was cut with this, and it's poisoned."

The healer took the knife from the guard and looked at it

closely. She raised her left hand and motioned to the blade. The weapon glowed faintly, purple sparks coming off of it. The healer nodded in understanding. The glow stopped abruptly. "It is good you brought her here so quickly."

The healer went to Portia's side. She looked at her injured arm, brows knit in concern. Drawing a pair of scissors from a nearby table, she cut the sleeve of Portia's jacket from her wrist to her shoulder, pulling back the material to expose the wounded arm. Portia could see tendrils of black and blue underneath her skin, winding their way up from the wound towards her neck. Where she had healed the wound, it did not look clean. Instead, it puckered in an ugly fashion, red cysts dotted along a white twisted scar.

"Who did this healing?" the healer asked, her mouth tight as she stared at the wound.

Portia swallowed. Aelric and Hilda had been adamant that she was not to explain her other skills to anybody, but if she didn't say anything now, she could die. Hopefully that would be reason enough. "I did it," Portia said, her voice a low whisper.

The healer frowned at Portia. "You were lucky this time, but next time get a healer—if you possibly can. You don't know what you're doing. This is not the way."

This confused Portia. She had healed herself many times in Valencia. It had been a valuable tool for her as an orphan in that city.

The healer placed her palm on Portia's forehead, pushing her head back down in the pillow. Portia felt the coolness on her forehead that spread out down through her body. Her arms and legs relaxed. The pain in her wounded arm faded. Her nausea receded enough for her to relax her stomach. Portia exhaled in relief.

The healer then focused on the wounded arm. She placed both hands on either side of the puckered scar on her arm. The white line glowed faintly red, then orange, then white-hot. The glow expanded up her arm and covered all the blue-black tendrils underneath the skin. Portia watched, feeling detached, as the wound opened up again. The red cysts disappeared, and the skin smoothed along the edge of what had been the scar. A clear liquid laced with traces of blood ran out of the wound into a shallow dish the healer had placed below her arm. Portia did not feel anything except for the cool relaxation from the healer's touch on her forehead. The liquid flow trickled, then stopped. The healer made a smoothing motion over the wound on Portia's arm and the edges of her flesh pushed together and blended into a smooth expanse of skin. There was no longer a scar. It was as if her arm had never been cut.

The glow from Portia's arm then spread to the rest of her body. It reduced in intensity but did not disappear completely. Portia's nausea disappeared completely. The fog in her head disappeared, as well as did the difficulty in her vision. The glow encasing her lasted for another second then stopped. Portia felt normal. She was completely healed.

Portia sat up while the healer removed the dish full of fluid and placed it on a nearby counter. Curiosity pulled at Portia. Was she doing all of her self-healing wrong? She removed the tattered remains of her jacket from her other arm and pulled up her sleeve. That was the side that had been bruised heavily from falling on the ice the previous day—bruises she had healed on her own. "Excuse me," Portia said, looking at the healer, "is this healed incorrectly as well?"

The healer returned to Portia's side and examined the proffered arm. "What was wrong with it?" she asked Portia.

"Bruising. I fell on it yesterday."

The healer grunted, touching the arm gently with her fingertips. Portia felt a tingle of magic as the healer probed her arm, examining Portia's healing work. "This is well done. I must admit I'm surprised, since I've not seen you before in the healing house."

"What did I do wrong with the other wound?" Portia quickly asked, wanting to distract the healer from any questions about what house Portia belonged to.

"Well, poison is a different thing entirely. It actively works against you—especially if it's a magic poison. You have to do two kinds of magic at the same time, one to fight the poison, and one to heal the wound. And you must do them in the correct order," the healer said. She removed her fingertips from Portia's arm. Going to a closet, she pulled a plain black kirtle from the cabinet. She tossed it to Portia.

Going to a coat closet, she pulled out a dark black coat which she also brought Portia. "It is too cold to go without a jacket. I'll have my assistant bring me another," she said, giving Portia a wink.

Portia gratefully took the jacket. It smelled of herbs and the healing house. "Can I go now?"

The healer gave her a shrug, then nodded her head at the

guards standing behind the platform Portia was sitting on. Portia turned to see them standing there, blocking the exit. She had forgotten all about the guards. She gave them a questioning look.

The smaller guard stepped forward. "We need you to come to the guardhouse. At the very least, you need to make a statement. We received no further instructions regarding you except to bring you here, so we're not releasing you until we get the go-ahead from the big boss." He spoke in a gruff manner, but not unkindly. Portia nodded her understanding.

They walked through the campus. The sun was setting—its baleful red glow covering the western sky and creating long shadows on the ground. Portia gave a little shiver in the cold air despite the warmth of the borrowed coat. It had been a long, eventful day. She wanted more than anything to rest.

They reached the guardhouse at the edge of campus. It was a large blue building, built of the same magically tinted bricks as all the other campus buildings but constructed in the style of a fortress, with tall turrets and a large metal gate that could lower in front of the main doors, trapping anyone inside.

Portia felt apprehension as they walked underneath the metal gate. But when they entered the building, her anxiety dropped. The inside was nothing like the outside. People bustled everywhere, and the hum of constant conversation was steadying. The building was full of small offices along the walls surrounding desks in a large common space. Guards were working at the desks and conversing in groups.

The guards led Portia to a small room off the main area of

desks. A serious-looking female guard sat at the desk, a stack of parchments in front of her. The woman nodded at the two guards, then motioned for Portia to have a seat at the chair next to the desk. "Hello, my name is Myra," the female guard said to Portia. She then pulled a quill pen from a well on the desktop.

The two guards who had escorted Portia stood by the doorway, one on each side. They did not sit down themselves. This made Portia a little uneasy. Portia gave them a small smile, trying to foster a sense of camaraderie. The smaller of the two guards smiled back, but the other remained stoic.

Myra pulled a parchment towards herself, her quill ready, then looked intently at Portia as she spoke. "We need your side of what happened. There has not been a death on campus in a long time. There has not been a violent death in even longer. Part of our procedure here is to take a statement right away. More than likely, it will be followed up with the truth cube in front of a tribunal. Do you understand?"

Portia nodded, swallowing. She hoped she would have a chance to speak to Professor Aelric or Professor Hilda before she was asked to speak in front of the truth cube. "Okay."

"Do you know the two who attacked you?"

Portia nodded again. "Yes. They're from Valencia."

"Valencia?" Myra said, a surprised expression on her face. She put her quill down. "That is far away—what were they doing here?"

"They were from my old... I was in a gang before. An orphan gang." Portia's cheeks flamed at the confession. She knew she shouldn't be ashamed. It was not her fault she had to be in a gang to survive, but somehow, she was still embarrassed. She pushed on, ignoring the heat in her cheeks. "The girl who died was the leader."

A soft whistle came from the direction of the door. Portia turned to see the friendlier guard looking at her. He was the one who had whistled. "You sure are levelheaded for a gang member. Not like anything I've ever met."

"Captain Ross," Myra said to the guard, a hint of reproach in her voice.

"I'm just saying…"

Myra closed her eyes slowly then opened them and nodded at Captain Ross. She then turned her attention back to Portia. "Captain Ross does have a point. The orphans in Coverack run wild. We've never had one successfully complete the Academy program. Usually their gang has something to say about it. Is that what happened here?"

"Yes… I think. Deyelna, that was the girl, did not want me in the gang but was enraged when I left. I don't understand it," Portia confessed.

"I think I do," Myra said as she wrote on the parchment. "I know that type."

Portia wanted Myra to explain it to her but didn't dare ask. It didn't feel like the right time.

"And who is the boy?" Myra asked.

Portia panicked at first, thinking she meant Mark, since she thought of Mark more as a boy than Peter. In her mind, Peter was too old and tall to be called a boy.

Myra prompted Portia while still continuing to write. "The one frozen to the ground?"

Relief flooded over Portia. "He was Deyelna's enforcer. It's what she called him."

"Looks like she needed to pick a better one," Captain Ross said softly.

"For our student, it's best that she didn't," Myra said, irritation on her face for being interrupted a second time.

Captain Ross did not respond, perhaps wisely taking a cue from Myra's expression, Portia thought.

Portia cleared her throat. She had to mention something about the possible others. "I think... I think they were working with some other people. Someone who created a distraction on the campus."

Myra stopped writing and looked at Portia with surprise. "How did you know about that?"

Portia couldn't give Mark away. She blurted out, "The dead girl told me." At their surprised looks, she quickly continued. "Before I... she was bragging about it."

Captain Ross whistled again. "Remind me to never be rude to you."

Myra flashed him an irate look. "Captain, I will *not* remind you again."

The captain looked down, suitably contrite. "My apologies."

The tense silence in the room, punctuated only by the sound of quill and parchment, was interrupted by a knocking on the doorframe. Portia turned to see a herald. He was dressed in a rich velvet overcoat with the royal insignia and knee-high leather boots.

The guards straightened in front of the herald, drawing themselves up at attention.

Myra looked up at the knocking then quickly put down her quill and stood up at attention herself. Portia followed suit, standing uncertainly.

The herald gave Myra a small nod. "Pardon the interruption, but I was told I could find Portia Harris here."

Myra gestured to Portia.

The herald then addressed Portia directly. "Are you Portia Harris?"

She nodded. "I am."

"Queen Lorica requests your presence immediately. Please come with me," he said.

Portia looked uncertainly at Myra and the guards. Myra waved her away. "We'll finish this later. Captain Ross will escort you."

Portia thought she could detect a hint of irritation on the face of the herald, but he said nothing to Myra. Instead, he backed out of the doorway so Portia could leave the room. He gestured for her to walk to the exit, falling in line behind her while Captain Ross brought up the rear.

17

Portia exited the guardhouse to see a beautiful, lacquered open carriage harnessed behind four large white horses in the driveway. The horses stomped and snorted, their breath frosty white in the cold air, creating clouds around the horses' heads. The moon shown down on the sight, taking Portia's breath away.

A driver held the reins of the horses while the herald held the door of the carriage open. It was huge. It could have sat four people. Portia climbed up into the carriage, taking the seat facing forward. The herald followed, taking the opposite seat. When Captain Ross tried to enter, the herald motioned for him to take one of the top seats in the rear—he would be allowed to escort them, but not in the main body of the carriage. Captain Ross scowled at this but took his seat and stared forward stoically.

With a flick of the reins, the driver let the horses go. The carriage leapt forward, drawn by the powerful horses. Portia fell back in her seat, surprised by the speed of the vehicle. "Oh."

The herald looked at her in concern. "Are you all right?"

"Yes, it's just that we're going so fast. I've never been in anything that's gone this fast in my life," she said, staring at the buildings go by as they passed through the city of Coverack, the driver weaving in and out between other carriages and wagons. More than one passerby leapt back to get out of the way of the speeding vehicle.

"This is nothing," the herald said, a small smile on his face. "The war carriages are even faster. And those horses are bred for speed."

Portia stared at him, her mouth a small circle. She caught herself and looked away, hearing a soft chuckle from the herald. "I've only been on wagons drawn by one horse. I never thought I'd ever ride something this fine," she said, touching the seat of the carriage. "It's the most beautiful thing I've ever seen."

"You've not seen the royal carriages yet then, I take it?" he asked.

"I might have," Portia said, thinking back to the carriage she'd seen on the road to Coverack.

"They're much as this, but larger. And fully enclosed." he said.

She nodded. That had been what she'd seen. "That would be nice for warmth," Portia said, drawing her jacket tight to her. The cold air blowing past her face chilled her.

Some of the aloofness left the herald's face. He unfolded a large thick blanket that was on the seat next to him and laid it over Portia's lap. "My apologies. I should've done this from the start."

Portia gratefully pulled up the blanket, trying to cover her arms and neck with it. She was sure she did not look dignified, but she didn't care. She was too cold to mind.

The herald looked shamefaced at his mistake. He leaned in with a conciliatory manner. "But it's not all pleasantries for the royal carriages. They are enclosed to prevent assassination attempts."

"Assassination!" It had never occurred to Portia that someone would try to harm the king and queen. "Do these attempts happen often? Who would do such a thing?"

"Not often, that is true. But violence has been tried in the past to previous head of state, so it makes sense to not take risks now."

"Oh." Portia felt she was so ignorant of the past. She had studied hours of history, but the more she studied, the more she realized she knew but just a fraction of what there was to know. She watched the buildings pass by, thinning, with larger and larger spaces between them. The houses had given way to large estates with shaped bushes and carefully shoveled driveways. The expense of the landscaping could be seen even under the deep snow.

The royal castle was at the far edge of the city, still within the gates but with a large space around it. The walls behind the castle were atop a large bluff that overlooked the sea, preventing an attack from the far side. Torches flamed along the road leading up to the castle, and upon its ramparts. It shone brightly in the night. The dark sea beyond the city walls spread as far as she could see and provided a backdrop for the bright lights of the castle.

The guards outside the castle opened the gates with a nod as the carriage approached, allowing it to pass through without slowing. Portia tried to get a closer look at the entrance, but they passed it too quickly. The main body of the castle soon distracted her.

The castle itself was a shimmering gray. Portia wondered if it was purple in the daylight.

"Am I to see the king and queen themselves?" Portia asked quietly, in awe, the magnitude of the event sinking in.

"The queen and the king consort," the herald corrected her. He looked at her more closely, surprised she did not know this. Portia squirmed under his attention.

They exited the carriage and were greeted by a butler who then escorted them through a large long hall. Tapestries and paintings filled the walls. The royal coat of arms was woven in beautiful silk threads on a large tapestry hanging over the door at the opposite end of the hall. Portia stared at it, drawing the herald's attention.

"The royal coat of arms," he explained.

She nodded, not comfortable speaking aloud in the butler's presence and in such an august space. Her stomach tightened. Anxiety filled her heart. She did not belong here. She feared being in trouble, for her lies to the Magic Academy staff, or worse yet, for her role in Deyelna's death. But there was nothing to be done but to continue on and face whatever was ahead of her.

They reached the doorway at the far end of the hall and

two servants opened the double doors in unison. The herald nodded at another servant standing just inside the next room. The servant tilted his head in acknowledgment and then turned, struck a staff to the floor three times, and announced in a booming voice, "Portia Harris."

Portia stood in the doorway and realized she was facing into the throne room. The queen and king consort sat on high-back chairs atop a dais. Stairs led down from the dais to the main floor. A few nobles stood below, flanked by a secretary at a table taking notes with a quill and parchment. Portia noticed Aelric and Hilda amongst the crowd. She was surprised to see them there, but it helped soothe her stomach. Even if Aelric didn't like her, she didn't think he would do anything to harm her. And she trusted Hilda.

The herald motioned for Portia to enter. She stepped into the room and continued walking towards the throne. Reaching the bottom of the stairs, she stopped and curtsied clumsily, not sure exactly how to do it.

"Please rise," Queen Lorica said, her voice gentle. Portia risked a glance up. The queen had tightly curled dark hair wrapped up in a high pile on her head and under a large golden crown. King Consort Aldis looked similar. He had a gentle smile that matched the queen's tone. "We are very pleased to meet you. We have never seen a Jack of Magic. Few people ever have."

Jack of Magic, Portia wondered. "I'm honored, Your Majesty... I think."

Queen Lorica tilted her head questioningly at Portia. No one else dared speak. "You think?"

"It's not that I'm not honored by you," Portia said in a rush, her cheeks glowing red, "but it's just that I... don't know what Jack of Magic means."

The queen frowned and then addressed Hilda and Aelric, "Professors, what are you teaching students these days? How can this girl not know what a Jack of Magic is?"

Hilda stepped forward and gave the queen small bow. "Your Majesty, this is Portia's first term at the Magic Academy. She has not had the benefit of a tutor growing up, so she is learning everything at once. I hope you can appreciate how unusual it is to have to know the term Jack of Magic at such a young age."

Queen Lorica acknowledged this with a nod. "This is true. Portia, being only the third Jack of Magic in all time, none of us are truly experienced in this."

"Thank you, Your Majesty," Hilda said. "Please rest assured this was part of the curriculum for this term. We had not gotten to it yet."

"That does nothing to ease our honored guest's present confusion. Please explain it now," the queen commanded.

Aelric and Hilda nodded at the queen. Aelric stepped forward, facing Portia. "People called Jack of Magic have only appeared twice before in our history. Both times they have been critical in saving the kingdom from ruin."

Portia tried to take in what Aelric was saying. Surely that couldn't apply to her. She couldn't save anyone; she was having a hard enough time surviving herself. They expected her to save the kingdom?

Hilda stepped forward to join Aelric. "The last Jack of

Magic occurred five hundred years ago. He was much needed to stop a necromancer from taking over the kingdom. It is doubtful the kingdom would have survived without him."

Queen Lorica nodded in agreement with this.

Aelric, not to be outdone, spoke again. "The one previous helped create the kingdom itself. More importantly, she set up magic to create Jacks of Magic when the kingdom was in need." He looked at her meaningfully. "Your very existence tells us there is danger coming. You will be needed. It is unfortunate you are so young. We can only hope we have time before events unfold.

"I'm too young?" Portia asked, confused how that mattered.

Hilda smile at her reassuringly. "It is not so much that you are too young, but more that we have not had the opportunity to help train you in skills that would both protect you and defend the kingdom. The Jack of Magic is powerful magic, but is no guarantee of success. You need to have all the skills we can put at your fingertips."

The queen stood then descended the stairs towards Portia. Portia could see how beautiful she was the closer she came. "Young Jack of Magic, it is certain that we will need you. Our oracles," Queen Lorica motioned to a group of advisers standing close by who bowed at her reference, "have foretold of dark events coming. One even dared speak of oncoming doom. They have been unable to see more clearly what is coming, but all of them, from the youngest to the oldest, have seen nothing like this before. We had hoped it was not of such magnitude as to need a Jack of Magic, but here you are, so we must face our danger and defeat it for the sake of the kingdom and our people. You must face our danger —you are our champion. We expect much of you."

Portia swallowed, uncomfortable both with what the queen was saying and her close proximity. "I will do my best," she said, her voice shaking. Portia's thrill at being a Jack of Magic suddenly took a nauseating turn at the thought of what might be expected of her. Her face heated as she realized she'd momentarily had the cowardly thought of how she could get out of it.

"I expect you will," Queen Lorica said. "You will receive the highest training available in the kingdom. You will learn things we do not teach the average magic user, even the most skilled of our Academy students. Training the Jack of Magic is the highest calling for the Academy."

Portia nodded.

"For all our sakes, I wish you a good—and thorough— training." The queen, followed by the king consort, exited the throne room, escorted by their personal guards, leaving the audience behind.

Portia breathed easier. She felt light-headed. Hilda noticed and grabbed both of Portia's hands within her own. "I know this is overwhelming, Portia, but you have skills beyond any other magic user, whether or not they are trained. You cannot run away the way you did from the gang in Valencia. This is different."

Portia wondered if Hilda could read minds. How did she know how badly Portia wanted to escape? The responsibility laid on her shoulders was beyond even her comprehension.

"You also cannot tell anybody of what you know here, at least not yet. There are those who would wish you to fail in your training, as incomprehensible as that may seem. Do you understand?" Aelric asked Portia. "I think after today, you have some idea of the stakes, both to the kingdom as well as to yourself personally. The anti-magickers will stop at nothing until you are killed—or they are."

Portia felt ill at this but calmly nodded acknowledgment. She couldn't imagine not telling Ella or Mia, her best friends and support in the Academy. Were they now in danger because they were around her? Perhaps she could get Aelric or Hilda to relent on that, or somehow convince them her friends would not betray their confidence. She was sure of it.

Aelric and Hilda escorted Portia out of the throne room. Not only was her place in the Magic Academy secure, she was a needed and important person in the kingdom. She couldn't have imagined this outcome when she had run away from Valencia. When they exited the castle, the night was pitch-black and the stars were twinkling over the kingdom. They helped her into the carriage, and as Portia journeyed back to the school she stared, unseeing, at the bobbing lights of ships in the harbor below the castle, and the yellow glow from the city's windows, all while her thoughts raced elsewhere. She couldn't wait to be back with the others at the house. Danger or not, she now had friends by her side.